THE LOVELAND FROG

AND THE

NARROW PATH

Mark D. Trollinger

Published by Myths and Malts Productions Chandler, AZ

The book is a work of fiction. The author drew the characters, incidents, and dialogue from his imagination and did not construe them as real. Some events from the original cryptid sightings have been retold, modernized, and at times, fictionalized.

This book includes the use of trademarks for realism. Product names, logos, brands, and other trademarks featured or referred to within this manuscript are the property of their respective trademark holders.

These trademark holders are not affiliated with the author or any of the author's representatives. They do not sponsor or endorse the contents, materials, or processes discussed within this book.

Drink responsibly and do not drink and drive

If you or a loved one need help with an alcohol problem, please reach out to SAMHSA's National Helpline: 1-800-662-HELP (4357).

The author will donate 15% of the sales from this book to the Loveland Learning Garden in Loveland, OH. I will make donations quarterly. See the *Field Notes* section at the back of the book for more details.

Cover by Nyssa Iniguez

Library of Congress Control Number: 2023908738

First Edition, first printing

Printed in the United States of America

ISBN: 9798988082835

also by Mark Trollinger

Texans Investigating Mysterious Entities Series:

The Chupacabra and the Bat Rastard

Champ and a Bit of Sunshine

The Red Ghost and a Chocolate Bunny

The Loveland Frog and the Narrow Path

Tegan Stone and the Gibson County Beast

The Ringdocus and a Guy on a Buffalo

Other Books:

Corrè

For Susana, Karmina, Jorge, Lydia, Linda, and Ginny

Also my great-grandparents,

Earl and Enid (aka Nene and Gramps)

TABLE OF CONTENTS

Chapter 1 1

Chapter 2 7

Chapter 3 25

Chapter 4 37

Chapter 5 49

Chapter 6 61

Chapter 7 83

Chapter 8 103

Chapter 9 119

Chapter 10 143

Chapter 11 157

Chapter 12 181

Chapter 13 197

Chapter 14 223

Chapter 15 241

Epilogue 251

Beer List 257

About the Author 263

CHAPTER 1

LITTLE MIAMI

A cool autumnal breeze blew listlessly through the trees along the embankment of the Little Miami River in the Cincinnati suburb of Loveland. Early in the evening, both the sun and crisp temperature plummeted. The susurrating leaves gently swayed, granting Björn Martin some relaxation as he trudged the shallow waters of this segment of the river. The twenty-two-year-old Danish student used the bat field technician internship as the final credits in the University of Cincinnati's Biological Science - Zoology degree program.

The evening's assignment was an investigation of the area south of Chateau Laroche, for tri-colored bats, or *Perimyotis subflavus,* as the textbooks labeled them. At three inches long and weighing approximately forty-six grams, it's one of the smallest American species often mistaken for a large moth. Classified as a microbat, it's identified by the individual strands of back hair displaying colors ranging from pale yellowish-brown to a dark reddish-brown, and visible in three distinct color bands along with its pink-hued forearms and a black wing membrane.

Once a common bat, the now endangered animal faces mounting threats including habitat loss, human interference, and white-nose syndrome. Difficult to locate because of its early-to-bed-late-to-rise hibernation habits, the university and local conservation groups sought to study the bats to address the declining population in known tri-colored typically hibernate colonies.

Recent sightings by local anglers, outdoor enthusiasts, and workers from a nearby straw and mulch company reported seeing nearly three dozen individuals in the area.

Björn used an ultrasonic bat detector to monitor general bat activity; remaining hopeful he would reach the intended target area before nightfall, fully set in. If he could beat total darkness, he could assess the potential effectiveness of the harp trap he intended to place in the area.

While the study's focus included an accurate census of the individuals, the researcher's primary goal sought to identify the microclimate preferences of tri-colored bats exposed to the fungus that causes white-nose syndrome. With this data, scientists hoped to reduce the devastating effects of the disease on the species.

Slowly traversing the waist-high water, Björn paused for a few moments under the train trestle near East Kemper Road after noticing a small colony of Mexican free-tailed bat, *Tadarida brasiliensis*, nesting in the corner near the pile cap. Although the largest colony of Mexican free-tailed bats was in Austin, Texas, the species was one of fourteen common throughout Ohio. Slowed by the steady, oncoming currents, he finally arrived at his small mid-river island target as the last fingers of the sun's rays disappeared.

Eagerly, he scurried to the edge of the island, evaluating the area for the trap's ideal location. The banks were thick with trees still fighting to keep the leaves. Some branches hung over the island's coast, somewhat reducing visibility.

One of two islands in this segment of the river, each was nature's way of reducing localized flooding. Their unique soil composition allowed the islands to absorb significant water during heavy rainfall, reducing the flood threat of people and property.

The sandy shore allowed Björn to extract his logbook and take notes in a last pause before setting the trap. Bent on a knee, he flipped through earlier entries, notating the time of day and weather. His jotting abruptly ceased when a noise disrupted his concentration, causing him to scan the terrain of the small island.

Listening intently, Björn detected a sound that reminded him of heavy feet moving through puddled water. It originated from what appeared to be a marsh that transitioned into a wildflower and tree-covered wetland meadow.

Björn stood to his feet to get a better look at the source of the sound, but between the tree cover and now total absence of sunlight, it was difficult to see anything. He took a few cautious steps further inland to catch a better look from higher ground. With a little higher elevation, he turned his head toward the direction of the neighboring mulch company to see if any employees were in the area. But it was after 6:00 p.m. and the workers there, as well as the plumbing company down the road, had already kicked off work and were likely killing time at the local watering hole over on Karl Brown Way, Narrow Path Brewing.

A nice cold beer *sounded* good, but he knew he would be on scene most of the night. Still, his gaze drifted away, and he cracked a smile. He *could* fantasize, right?

A repeat of the unidentified noise drew his attention back to his surroundings. Was someone else here on the island? That theory felt unlikely, but what else could it be? Most of the animals in the area were birds, squirrels, and groundhogs. Certainly not large enough to make that loud of a sound.

With caution, he reached into his backpack, scanned the horizon, and extracted a flashlight. Now that the sun was gone, the flashlight provided enough illumination to improve his sight. As he walked closer toward the sound, Björn panned the area and slowly inched closer, hoping not to disturb the sound's author. As he continued deeper, he drew back in surprise as many of the fallen trees caused him to think he saw something. A naturally created Rorschach test of unknown images in every exposed trunk.

He emerged from the trees and stared at a small clearing ahead on the island's Eastern side. Squinting his eyes, he felt certain he saw three figures crouched down. Again, he strained his eyes, attempting to solve the puzzle in his mind that caused him to think they were giant frogs.

The unknown figure arched its head back and sniffed the air, stood erect, and turned toward the young intern. Björn continued to fight through his thoughts. There were definitely three of… Whatever they were, and they were about sixty yards away. As they stood in a bipedal position, he could tell from their muscular hind legs that whatever they were, they appeared to scamper on two legs.

Björn continued to watch on, as two of the creatures leaped from the island edge across to the embankment in one bound. The third remained quietly glaring into the bright beam of light generated by the flashlight. The animal squinted through the brightness and locked eyes on Björn. Immediately upon the flashlight's glare striking the animal in the eyes, Björn saw eyes that appeared to be a solid green, with no pupils. He felt an evil quiddity present in the air.as he stared in disbelief.

Breaking its staring contest with the human, the creature produced a wand-like light-emitting device that surprised Björn with its brightness. Both the student and the creature suffered from temporary blindness, but instinctively retreated in opposite directions.

Working as an animal field technician and being a student of zoology, Björn learned to observe details and accurately recount any encounters with wildlife in their natural habitat. He was familiar with many animals, not only native to the area, but in many regions around the world, yet what he saw that night was behind his explanation. He saw it, right? But what he saw, or thought he saw, didn't compute with anything he could recall. He thought back on the physical characteristics he observed but couldn't identify an animal that fit the description: between three and four feet tall, over fifty pounds, and possibly greenish leathery skin. And its face. The first impression that stood out to him was a frog. But with sharp teeth?

His training allowed him to remain calm and fearless in the situation, but those skills were failing him now. How could he trust his other skills were working correctly? A strange feeling and rush of energy rushed over him. There was no time to think about assessing his skill set now. What he was certain of was his willingness to listen and accept that his fight-or-flight response was kicking in and *flight* was winning.

Björn thought, as he rushed toward the nearest embankment, *Maybe that cold beer was indeed calling him.* Especially after what he observed. Maybe tonight called for *two* cold beers.

CHAPTER 2

THE JACKALOPE

Tyson Carr, Kareem Ortiz, Tegan Stone, and Carson Quinn walked briskly down an Austin sidewalk, attempting to reach their scheduled event in time.

"We're cutting it close," said Kareem, looking down at his watch.

Ty took a step back and held the door open for his friends.

"Wow, there are a lot more people here than I expected," Tegan said as she entered first.

She paused and looked around a large, open room.

"What a huge turnout! I wasn't expecting this many people. Especially on a work night," replied Kareem.

"They wanted to witness Carson getting his hands on a jackalope!" Ty jested.

"I would never have found it without your guidance," Carson professed to Ty as they made their way to their seats.

"It's a great, unexpected day! I didn't think we'd ever see the day Carson captured the jackalope," joked Kareem.

A young woman with her blonde hair worn in a bun approached the group, carrying a tray of hamburgers. The smell of the burgers reached the table's occupants milliseconds before the server did.

"The 'Bama burger for you, sir," she proclaimed, handing a plate to Ty. "The chipotle bacon cheeseburger for the lady," she noted, handing a plate to Tegan. "Honey-jalapeno bacon for you," she said, handing the third plate to Kareem. "And for the birthday boy, the Chupacabra burger," she announced to Carson.

"A chupacabra and a jackalope all in the same night? What could be a better birthday celebration?" Carson said to the group as the server dropped off the last of the food.

"Are you still okay with your drinks?" the server asked.

"Yes, we are good for now, thank you," replied Carson.

""'Kay, I'll check back in a bit," she said as she turned. She disappeared into the crowded room and headed toward the kitchen.

"My research only revealed positive feedback about this place," stated Kareem as he looked around the establishment dubbed *Austin's favorite and most famous dive bar with incredible food.*

"I have wanted to come here for a while," replied Carson.

"I always see it listed as one of the top burgers in Austin, and of course the name the Jackalope attracted me. Not only do I get the elusive jackalope, but they also named a burger after our first team cryptid. How cool is that?"

"That giant saddled jackalope in the restaurant's front is begging for a selfie. And around the corner is one of my favorite Tex-Mex spots near the office. The Chupacabra Cantina y Taqueria," added Kareem.

"That's a good amber. Sweet and malty, light and hoppy," reported Carson, taking a sip from his pint of Thirsty Goat Amber.

"Great pairing with your burger. A thirsty goat and a chupacabra go naturally together," observed Ty prior to taking a sip from his Sputnik Imperial Stout.

"A match made in heaven, but this Stash IPA remains one of my favorite IPAs," stated Kareem.

"Their Power & Light Session IPA is one that's a staple in my refrigerator," added Tegan

"For the record, this isn't my first jackalope," replied Carson. "The other day, I received beer mail from Bobbye out in Phoenix. Remember her from our trip to World of Beer and the concert afterward at the Yucca Tap Room? Well, we've stayed in contact. She's my beer plug in Phoenix and sent me a six-pack of Jackalope Pils from the Shop Beer Company for my birthday," he stated.

"Why don't we have a beer plug from Phoenix? I enjoyed what they're doing with the beer market out there," responded Ty.

"Maybe we could get that Vanilla Heat guy?" pondered Kareem. "He was awesome."

"Yeah, I'd love to have a beer with him again," replied Tegan.

"Did Bobbye send anything else with the Jackalope?" asked Tegan.

"Indeed - a few cans of a German Pilsner from Helio Basin called Chupacabra Logga, a DIPA from Wren House called Dreamy Draw, and their triple IPA, Mercury Mine," reported Carson.

"Damn, those names take me back to our Phoenix investigation," responded Kareem.

"You should see the art on the Dreamy Draw can. There's the dam on the front and a UFO on the back," revealed Carson.

"No shit? Now I need to get my hands on one!" exclaimed Tegan.

"I've got a few cans of each. Next time you're over, I'll hook you up," said Carson.

"Whichever one of you picked this place for Carson's birthday, I approve," said Ty, biting into his Bama burger.

Tegan raised her hand to accept credit for her role in the birthday planning.

"This pulled pork and slaw takes me back to my childhood," Ty said.

"I thought you grew up in Illinois?" questioned Kareem. "Pulled pork and slaw is a southern thing."

"I did, and you are correct, but my momma is from Greenwood, Mississippi. And this is how she used to fix pulled pork sandwiches. Topped with slaw, cheddar cheese, onions, pickles, and spicy mustard," reminisced Ty.

"This chipotle bacon cheeseburger reminds me of my youth, too," replied Tegan. "We had little growing up, so there was a lot of lunch meat and pimento cheese. This burger uses pimento cheese instead of sliced cheese, but otherwise it's a great traditional bacon cheeseburger. The chipotle mayo gives it a nice kick."

"In Mexico, we had a lot of spicy food. This burger has jalapeño jack cheese, bacon, pickles, a spicy mayo, and an added kick from this honey-jalapeño sauce. I love it," replied Kareem as he took a large bite.

"How's the chupacabra?" asked Ty.

"A little messy, but great. Perfectly cooked, the waffle fries are crisp, but it packs a powerful bite," Carson said.

Realizing the similarity to their first team hunt, he raised his glass toward his friend.

"No offense, Ty."

"None taken. Our first investigation was a little messy, and that chupacabra had a nasty bite too," he said, rubbing a phantom pain from his shoulder at the reminder.

"I've never had a burger quite like this - barbacoa de chivo, salsa verde, pepper jack cheese, jalapeños, pickles, and a ghost chili aioli. My taste buds are in overdrive with every bite," Carson replied.

The server returned through the large brick arch and passed by the giant jackalope as she arrived back at their table. "How's everyone doing? Enjoying those burgers? Another round of drinks?" she asked.

"I think we'll do one more before heading next door," said Carson.

"One each of the same beers?" she asked as the group nodded in agreement.

"Let's not forget the selfie with the jackalope up front," replied Kareem. "We have to commemorate your birthday!"

"Hell yeah! And I'm going to ride it. Cowboy-style," Carson pledged.

Thirty-five minutes flew by with the group talking about cryptid investigation adventures, funny happenings from prior trips, and enjoying the company of close friends with common interests.

Exiting the Jackalope, the group stepped into the crisp evening air and began the fifty-foot journey to the Chupacabra Cantina y Taqueria.

"Don't worry about driving tonight. I already called Jourdyn, and she's coming to pick us up later tonight. I have to call her when we're ready, and she'll be here ten minutes later," reported Tegan.

"Why didn't she join us tonight?" asked Ty.

"She and her boyfriend already had prior plans," replied Tegan. "But she'll be done with her event before we're finished."

"Boyfriend? I didn't know she was dating," replied Carson.

"Apparently they just started dating a couple of months ago. I haven't met him. I think he's in the military and they met online," replied Tegan.

"Maybe I should give online dating a try. Who knows, maybe there's someone out there even for me," Carson responded.

"Not to be a downer on your birthday, but I think you still have a lot to work through before you're ready to get entangled with someone else," stated Ty.

"Probably right," said Carson. "But we can put aside those demons for now and have fun tonight."

"The night is young," Ty said as he slapped Carson on the upper shoulder. "Let's see if the old man can keep up tonight," he chuckled.

"I can still hold my own with a night on the town," responded Carson. "And who you calling old? I'm only a few months older than you," he retorted.

"Still older," shot down Ty.

"Since she has handled the drive home," began Kareem. "It's time to kick this party up a notch! Shots! Shots! Shots!" he exclaimed with a fist-pumping motion.

Soon Tegan and Ty repeated the gesture.

"Fine with me!" answered Carson. "Tomorrow is a light day at the office - our regular Friday team meeting and some file organization for me," he stated.

"My day is pretty light too," responded Ty as he opened the Chupacabra's door.

It was dark inside the Chupacabra, with the only natural light sources being along the storefront. The cantina's only illumination came from behind the bar and some spaced recessed lighting along a large brick wall.

The wall furnishings featured local paintings of Dirty Harry, Vicente Fernandez, a green-skinned topless woman in a bed of tomatoes, a guitar flocked on each side by artistic roosters, and a chupacabra playing an accordion around a campfire while a scantily clad woman danced while the other wall contained multiple televisions broadcasting sporting events. The bar turned off the television's sound because it was karaoke night. A sizeable crowd was already enjoying some of the first singers of the evening, who sounded as if they began pregaming much earlier in the day. Unlike the breweries the group visited, the Chupacabra felt more like a jumpin' mini club.

The cantina promoted nightly drink specials throughout most nights, making it a popular mid-week drinking spot for many who lived or worked in the area. There was no vacancy at the bar's blue metal seats, and a sea of people stood behind, congesting the area. A nearby row of tables was also near capacity, but fortunately, a suitable table for four opened as another group vacated it. Carson and the gang moved into the seats before the server could clear the table.

"This might surprise you guys, but instead of beer, I'm going to change it up tonight," said Carson. "Although they have a good selection of draft and bottled beer, this place's popularity comes from their selection of over fifty different tequilas," he said, looking over the options.

"How about that one?" he asked, pointing a long finger toward the dusty chalkboard menu. "If we're going big, the board says that's the strongest drink on Sixth."

"A two-drink-per-person limit? Must be a reason," said Tegan.

"The Texas Tornado is fine by me," added Carson. "Who's in?" he asked, nodding as each friend raised a hand.

As a break in the singing occurred, the server approached the table.

"Evening," she said as she noticed a small birthday hat on Carson's head, placed there by Tegan. "Looks like we're celebrating tonight?"

"Yes, with a couple of rounds of Texas Tornados to start," replied Carson.

"That's easy," she replied. "Are you also singing tonight?" she asked as she placed a karaoke song list on the table.

"Not for me… and you'll thank me for that," replied Ty.

"Speak for yourself," answered Kareem, clearing his throat.

"I've been known to sing a time or two," stated Tegan.

"And the birthday boy?" asked the server, awaiting a response from Carson.

"Depends on how strong those tornadoes are," he answered with a hearty chuckle.

"Strongest on Sixth," the server responded.

"That's what it says on the sign," Carson verified.

"We'll get you started, and I will leave the song list and the drink menu here," she said, placing two laminated documents on the table as she cleared the remaining items from the prior customers.

Minutes later, she returned to the table with a round brown serving tray containing four glasses, each filled with a pink frozen margarita, garnished with a lime wedge and a black straw protruding from the top. The glass was icy to the touch as each friend accepted the beverage handed to him or her by the server.

Carson took a sip to see if the drink lived up to its hype. His immediate reaction reflected the high booze content and bit of sour fruit, but soon he nodded his head in agreement with local reviews that suggested it was one of the best margaritas in town. The cantina DJ played a perfect blend of old and new school songs on a laptop in between karaoke participants. It wasn't long before the group felt the initial wave of the power of the Texas Tornado.

"Damn, this is fantastic," said Kareem. "Good call on the margaritas tonight."

"Before we become professional storm chasers and get in too much of a whirlwind, let's toast the birthday boy. Let's get a group selfie to remind us tomorrow when we're hungover from blacking out," suggested Ty.

The server returned and took the photo for the group as she dropped off extra napkins and checked to make sure everyone liked their drink. The table replied with satisfaction as they made goofy faces and hand signals for the photo. The flash went off, blinding them in the dimly lit corner of the bar.

"A second round of Tornados?" she asked, receiving non-verbal approval in response.

A male patron, wearing a yellow button-up dress shirt - unbuttoned at the top two buttons, a loosened orange and white striped tie, short black hair attempting to hide a receding hairline, and bright green fashion glasses took the stage. The group could tell he arrived for happy hour after work and hadn't left. He grabbed the microphone, stumbled as he turned to face the audience, and began a slow and pitiful rendition of *Every Rose Has Its Thorn*. Within seconds, the group turned its attention back to each other and attempted to drown out the barely intelligible lyrics from the man, who, if he were sober, would be embarrassed by his performance. The server arrived with the second round of Tornados to help their cause.

"So...," began Tegan as she took a sip from the fresh drink. "Speaking of scary stuff, have you guys seen the uptick in stories about the Michigan Dogman?"

"Not only there, but I saw a Dogman story from Florida last week," replied Kareem.

"They're all over. Down in Louisiana there was a sighting reported to the North American Dogman Project website," added Ty. "It's like Dogman sightings are as popular now as Bigfoot."

"They've been around a long time. Remember, on MonsterQuest, Linda Godfrey described research dating back to 1936. Not to mention her own research of the Beast of Bray Road in the nineties up in Elkhorn, Wisconsin," chipped in Carson.

"When I think of Louisiana, I think Rougarou," said Tegan.

"As many sightings as we are seeing in the news, we might want to add that to our case files and run an investigation," suggested Kareem.

"I have seen an uptick in released scientific evidence of cryptids," stated Ty. "There was a study from scientists attempting to collect DNA from multiple sites to identify Loch Ness sightings, the FBI released files related to Bigfoot, and even the Merriam-Webster Dictionary added the word cryptid to its list of words. A pretty exciting few months from a research standpoint."

"The government and FBI's knowledge of Bigfoot and several other cryptids shouldn't be a surprise after what we found down in Phoenix," replied Kareem.

"I like to think that our work has helped fuel the interest in mysterious creatures," Tegan responded. "The chupacabra gained a lot of attention and it drew people to the visitor's center in Elmendorf in large numbers. When we brought attention to Champ up in Burlington, it showed the environmental connection between our world and cryptids."

"Our investigations have been challenging a lot of beliefs and showing people that these creatures exist. Not to mention the whole dark arts activity and aliens we uncovered when investigating the Red Ghost out in Phoenix," said Carson, noticing the bad karaoke singer had moved on to an equally horrible attempt at Frank Sinatra's *My Way*. Shaking his head, he returned his attention to the conversation. "Those files from Phoenix are some things I still need to reorganize in the office," Carson concluded.

"I think it's time for a shot," suggested Ty. "I saw on the tequila menu they have a Tequila Rose and Blavod Vodka drink."

"What's that make?" asked Tegan.

"You'll like it. It's called the Black Rose. It's a mix of the strawberry cream from the Tequila Rose with the shadowy black vodka," replied Ty. "Not only does it taste good, but the outstanding swirling gives a fun visual effect. Perfect for someone in the mysterious realm of work we do."

"I'm impressed," replied Kareem. "I didn't picture you to be into sweet, fruity strawberry shots," he said with a smile.

The server returned to the table with four shots of Black Rose. The friends took the drink and marveled at the pink and black swirled concoction in front of them. As they brought the shots together for the toast, the DJ announced the next singer.

"Next up, Kareem. Kareem Ortiz to the stage," the DJ said.

"Shit, I'm up!" Kareem announced as they clinked the shot glasses together. He downed the contents. "You guys pick the next round of shots while I sing," he said as he walked toward the back of the bar.

"This is going to be… something," replied Tegan as she watched her friend step on stage in preparation to sing. She pulled out the cellphone and prepared to take a video of what was sure to be a spectacle.

Seconds later, the music started and Kareem, with his back to the audience, spun around and started singing.

"Hey sister, go sister, soul sister, go sister," he sang, and then repeated.

"He's not…" started Carson.

"Yes, he is… *Lady Marmalade*… oh and there are dance moves!" Tegan said, as her eyes grew wide and her smile wider.

"You know he's seen *Moulin Rouge* like a hundred times," added Ty.

The table remained silent while Tegan recorded what might be future blackmail material for most people, although she knew Kareem didn't embarrass easily. He would own his performance and ask her to email it or tag him in the video if she posted it online. As Kareem concluded and returned to the table, the warm reception and smattering of applause he received surprised Ty and Carson. But not Tegan. She knew he would slay it.

Kareem was exuberant when he returned to the table, high off his performance. He enjoyed the attention and admiration of a crowd. Out of breath, he pulled out the chair and took a seat. He and Tegan turned toward each other and gave a little smirk-shrug gesture, showing they both understood he was the top performer of the night.

"My turn to pick the shot," said Tegan. Looking over the menu, she selected a layered Kahlua, Baileys Irish Cream, and Grand Marnier shot called the B-52, as Kareem mumbled, *Gitchi, gitchi, ya-ya, da-da* and continued to hum the tune of his song choice.

"Sounds like a good choice," graded Carson.

"I'm about to sing *Love Shack*, that's why," she added as the DJ announced her to the stage.

"Tegan Stone, to the stage."

She placed the order with the server, then ran up to the stage to perform one of her favorite songs. It was one she always sang at karaoke nights. Kareem returned the video favor with his phone, knowing she would do well. Not as well as him, but much better than the average person in attendance would do.

As she sang, "*Bang, bang, bang, on the door, baby*", Kareem stood, still filming, and yelled, "*Knock a little louder*" along with a handful of tipsy customers. Moments later, they followed it by screaming, "*I can't hear you!*"

The drinks arrived as Tegan concluded and dashed back to the table into the open arms of Kareem. As the two embraced, they hopped around a little. Each took their seat and downed the liquid inside the shot glass. The drink's name mirrored the name of the band that made the song famous.

Carson rubbed his head as the drinks from the evening caught up with him. His eyes drooped, and it was clear he was feeling the onset of fatigue that accompanies a night of heavy drinking.

"Not so fast, buddy. Time for my round," added Kareem.

Carson looked at his friend, a little nervous as to his choice of drink.

"Is it something… *Marmalade*?" quipped Carson.

"No, something spicy. Like me!" Kareem shot back. "Hmm. You have reposado?" he asked, intrigued by the menu. "Of course you do. You have fifty tequilas!"

He ran his finger down the menu and stopped at El Vocho, a shot of reposado tequila with a spicy chaser comprising pineapple, cilantro, mint, and jalapeño. It combined a slight sweetness with the vicious spicy kick… like Kareem.

"Four of 'em, coming right up," replied the server.

Good thing we hired Jourdyn, Carson thought as he pondered the rapidly approaching end of the evening. Then they each clinked the glasses and chugged the tequila first, followed by the spicy chaser. The hotness of the green chaser caused all four of them to react with a tongue out, attempting to calm the spicy down through the touch of fresh air. It was unsuccessful.

"Okay, the last one's on me," replied Carson. "Birthday boy, time to end this," he said, looking up at the group, uncertain they could finish one more. "Let's go back to when Ty and I were in college. Remember those days? Those were fun times… and when we were having fun, I always liked a flaming Dr. Pepper!" reminisced Carson.

"God, I haven't had one of those in years," Ty replied.

The server brought four pints of Architetto Ruffini Italian Pilsner, accompanied by four shots of 151 rum topped with an amaretto float.

"Are you guys ready?" asked the server.

Carson and the group nodded. He looked at Tegan, then said, "Time to call Jourdyn."

He looked at Kareem.

"Get the check." He looked at Ty.

"Brings back some old memories, buddy!"

After a head nod from each, the server lit the shots on fire and backed off as four eager hands rushed in, grabbed the shot glass, dropped it in the beer, and chugged as the drinks' excess spilled down the sides of their mouths. In unison, each raised a right forearm to their mouths and wiped it clean.

Carson shot a solo finger gun at the group. "I'll be right back," he said as he turned and headed to the restroom. The server returned to the table with the check as Tegan dropped the company's credit card on top.

"Damn, what a fun night," said Kareem.

"Yeah, I think nothing can top this night. It's been a while since we turnt up like this," replied Tegan.

As Carson exited the restroom, he paused after he noticed a slight relief in the wall with a few decorations. One such decoration was a dusty wooden guitar bearing cobwebs. Carson stared at it for a second, then with guitar in hand, disappeared back toward the bar floor. Ty, Kareem, and Tegan were too busy talking to each other to notice Carson reentered the room, turned, and lumbered toward the stage. They only stopped talking to look up when they heard the strum of a guitar string. Their mouths were agape as they saw Carson sitting on a stool on stage with the dusty guitar in his hands. He strummed the strings again.

"Wow, that's bad!" Carson said into the microphone as he adjusted the seat's level. He chuckled and looked down at the guitar before giving it another slow, pitiful strum.

"Yeah, that's… damn… that's out of tune," he said, followed by a lengthy pause. "So, anyways… Here's *Wonderwall*," he said as he clumsily attempted to strum the Em, G, D, A7sus4 chords to open the song.

Tegan silently raised the cellphone and clicked record.

CHAPTER 3

AIN'T AFRAID OF NO GHOST

The sound of boots scuffing against the wooden floor echoed as Parker Hickman entered the large, open second-floor ballroom of Chateau Laroche. He walked through the dark room with the only light emanated from the night vision glow on the screen from his Bell & Howell camcorder. His camcorder panned the entire room, Parker hoping to pick up mysterious movement or perhaps capture a disembodied voice in the audio playback. He and the rest of the Porkopolis Paranormal Society were excited to have the opportunity for a nighttime investigation in the reportedly haunted Loveland Castle.

Twenty-five-year-old Parker grew up watching all the classic ghost hunting shows and jumped at the chance to join the paranormal group last summer. Every time the group went out for an investigation, he felt a heavy mixture of excitement and anticipation rolled up in one. He was still learning the ropes to investigating the unknown and keeping his nerves in check.

"Buck to Parker," said a voice over the walkie-talkie. It was the voice of Buck Cane, one of the team leaders of the Porkopolis Paranormal Society.

"Go for Parker."

"You have anything up there?" asked the team leader.

"No. Pretty quiet up here. You?"

"Nothing down here, either. I'm going to meet up with the others," announced Buck.

"I'll be right down," replied Parker.

"Meet in the dungeon?" asked Buck.

"Roger," said Parker, before returning the device to a holster on his hip. He looked out of the narrow windows overlooking the terraced gardens where the castle's builder used to grow fruits and vegetables year-round in hotbeds heated by railroad lanterns. He saw nothing outside, and moved to descend the stairs to the main level, then further into the downstairs dungeon, where the rest of the group awaited.

"Tonight's been quiet," replied Buck, an experienced paranormal investigator who founded the group over ten years ago with Patti Pennington. Buck and Patti were never a couple, although most people, including their friends, speculated. They had many common interests and spent a lot of time together chasing ghosts in dark corners, hoping to answer the question, *What happens when we die?*

The fourth member of the team was another newbie, although not as new as Parker. Jocasta Jagger was in her mid-thirties and joined the group three years ago after a divorce, and her husband moving off to parts unknown. Together, the team investigated many locations rumored to be haunted in the southwest Ohio/northern Kentucky area.

Buck and Patti were well known in the local paranormal community and had a solid reputation of ethics and credibility. They had a decent-sized following on social media and occasionally opened the investigations up to a few locals who wanted to experience an honest paranormal investigation. Tonight, it was the four of them exploring the Loveland Castle for the first time.

"We should circle back to that domed bedroom. I thought I saw a shadow, but got nothing conclusive on the camera," said Patti.

"You and Jocasta take that room, and Parker and I will explore this dungeon," suggested Buck.

The women returned to the stairs and headed to the upstairs bedroom, while the men fanned out in the dungeon.

"These suits of armor look outstanding," stated Parker. "It's weird to see a medieval-looking castle in Ohio. I have to admit I don't know the origins of this place, and with it being tucked down this steep, winding road, I haven't seen it in person much," admitted Parker.

"Amazing story," responded Buck. "The builder of the home, Old Man Andrews, is one of the suspected ghosts I hope to run into tonight."

"You think he's here?" asked Parker.

"Wouldn't doubt it. He poured his soul into this place. Built the whole thing with his hands. That amount of dedication I figure would be hard to give up in the end," said Buck.

"Built it himself?" questioned the young investigator.

"Yeah -they say he went through 32,000 milk cartons, 2,600 bags of cement, and over 56,000 buckets of stone to build this place," answered Buck.

"How'd he come up to build a castle here?" inquired Parker.

"If you talk to an annalist, back in the 1920s Andrews was involved with the boy scouts and a Sunday school teacher. Back in the 1920s, the *Cincinnati Enquirer* offered plots of land along the river to anyone who paid a one-year subscription in advance. He was a troop leader of about twelve boys. He and a few parents purchased eleven lots from the paper. They liked to camp along the banks of the Little Miami and became frequent visitors. So much so they started leaving their camping equipment there. However, over time, they started losing a lot of their stuff, either from people stealing it, animals running off with it, or the weather ruining it. Therefore, Harry erected two tents, one for their equipment and one for shelter. Since they were a scout group and groups usually had names, they called themselves the Knights of the Golden Trail," added Buck.

"That must have been a lot of fun. I was in the scouts for a brief period, but had to give it up," responded Parker.

"Harry also had a high IQ, allowing him to write, read, and speak seven languages fluently and hold several degrees. He studied at Colgate University and in France at Toulouse University, which caused him to be obsessed with medieval architecture. In WW1, everyone thought he died, but he survived the war and received a knighthood for his bravery as a medic on the front lines. That's where he first caught the idea of knights and the origin of the Knights of the Golden Trail began," said Buck.

"They thought he died? But he didn't?" asked Parker.

"He contracted spinal meningitis and became paralyzed, blind, and unable to speak. It was so bad they declared him dead and sent his body to the morgue. It wasn't until later when doctors performed an autopsy they realized something wasn't right because Harry's mouth bled. The doctors were like, *wait a minute, dead men don't bleed!* They were unsure what to do, so they gave Harry an experimental drug called adrenaline. That caused his heart to beat irregularly. The military discharged him after doctors reported they were certain he wouldn't survive more than a few days. He ended up living until 1981 - over sixty more years!" told Buck.

"That's quite a story. And that's when he built this place?" asked Parker.

"Yes, the troops had their tents, but Harry thought what a knight needed was a castle. He set out to build one on the land. He started in 1929 and worked for over fifty years on it. The name Château Laroche comes from the name of the military hospital in the Chateau La Roche in southwest

France, where he served during the First World War. In French, the name meant *rock castle*. Today, most people call it Loveland Castle," finished Buck.

"What happened to the place after he died?" continued Parker.

"Eventually it became his residence, and he continued to have troop meetings and Bible lessons on Sundays, so when he died, he willed it to the Knights of the Golden Trail. A volunteer unit of Knights still looks after the place," stated Buck.

"That's interesting. I wouldn't be surprised if he is still walking these halls… although we haven't found him tonight," said Parker.

"There have been sightings by some of the Knights who convinced themselves it is Harry Andrews' ghost. But Harry's not the only one here," Buck segued.

"He's not?" questioned Parker.

"They say a woman believed to have died during a moonshine explosion in a nearby cave is often spotted walking across the river behind the castle, or even sitting in the seats in that courtyard out there," stated Buck.

"That so?" mumbled Parker.

"She's the White Lady. They say there is also a Viking Entity here likely attached to one of the many antique swords Andrews held in his extensive collection," replied Buck. "Many of them are housed right here in the dungeon. Keep your eyes peeled," he warned.

He walked toward the opposite corner of the room, distracted by increased flashing lights representing EMF readings coming from his device.

"Cool. Check that out. I'm going to walk this way and see what I find," shouted Parker.

He walked along the wall in the darkened dungeon, feeling for armor and other displays stored in the museum. Resting his hand on the wall, he felt something slip, and it surprised him to find a hidden door that led outside to the garden. Parker pushed the wall open wider and turned to look back at Buck as he stepped into the cool night air.

The night air was crisp, but at least it was fresh. Parker admired the lush garden, including fruits and vegetables. Buck briefed him earlier in the evening. Harry Andrews designed all the structures in the Castle, which appear to include secret passages. It also contained hotbeds that allowed the vegetables to grow all year old, despite the cold Ohio winters. Harry created his own design by which the railroad lanterns heated the beds.

Parker reached his hand out and touched the petals of several flowers and bushes as he walked by. The bright moon overhead helped provide enough visibility to allow him to see where he was going. Exploring the ground further, he didn't hear any paranormal screams or feel any telekinetic activity. He continued to walk through the garden, hoping for some groundbreaking evidence, when he noticed another arched path leading toward a hidden staircase descending to the driveway below. He took a few steps down, and then stopped, listening to the sound of the nearby Little Miami River. Realizing he was close and remembering a large yard on the other side of the driveway as they drove to the Castle, he walked down and had a smoke.

As he left the rocky steps of the castle behind him, his feet crunched on the limestone rocks placed out front to serve as a parking area. A few more crunches under his Doc Martens, and he reached the grassy edge of the yard. A narrow path led down to the river's embankment.

He decided not to explore the path, but to sit down on the top of a wooden picnic table in the yard and have his smoke. He placed the cigarette in his mouth, lit the end, and took a drag. He sat up, exhaled the smoke, and scanned the nearby area. He looked at their vehicles parked in the rocky driveway, then at the edge of the bank, focusing on the sound of the water. He drifted towards a little bend in the yard ahead. That's when he heard a rustling in the bushes and thought he detected movement.

"That's it Andrews! Maybe you *are* out here!" said Parker aloud as he picked the camcorder up with one hand and draped the cigarette from one corner of his lip, hurrying toward the suspected spirit. Finishing another drag, he reached up and removed the cigarette from his lips, flicking it to the side in a puddle as he continued at a little quicker pace.

From the moon's shine, the path ahead was well-light. Enough light that allowed Parker to question if he saw a visual of the ghost ahead. There was something there, but it wasn't Andrews. It sounded like multiple spirits moving around. Now cigarette-free and sporting a sly grin, he held the camcorder in position and started recording as he looked through the green lit-display.

"What the?" Parker announced as he stared into the viewfinder and noticed the image looking back at him. He held the camcorder down as he looked up at the path, trying to get a visual from the naked eye.

It was something. Something solid. He looked back down into the viewfinder and moved closer toward the unknown object. He picked up the pace into a slow jog, then a little faster. Faster still until he became airborne, thanks to a rock extruding from the grassy ground. As Parker hit the ground, he tried to look for the source. He also could only watch as the camcorder flew before landing hard on the ground, landing on its side. The camera was undamaged, and the video continued to roll, albeit somewhat obstructed by blades of high grass.

Then Parker saw a bright light that caused him, even laying on his stomach on the damp ground, to close his eyes and bury it into the thick grass below his body. When Parker closed his eyes, he felt as though he fell asleep and his head nodded forward. When we opened his eyes, he didn't feel like it was a quick nod of the head. It felt longer.

He pushed himself off the ground and dragged a dusty hand across the top of his head as he attempted to shake the sudden drowsy feeling. He habitually looked down at his left wrist to check the time. It surprised him to see the watch show twenty minutes had passed.

"What the hell happened?" he asked himself. He walked over and picked up the camera, turning it around to look at the viewing panel on the back. "Looks like it's broken," he said as he continued to stare and rotate the camera.

"Maybe the battery's dead," he speculated. "I gotta get back with the others and check this footage. We should have extra batteries inside," he said, as he made his way toward the Castle.

Back inside the castle, Parker found the others gathered in the entryway.

"There you are," said Jocasta. "We were wondering."

"I don't know what happened out there," admitted Parker. "I was outside, thought I saw something, then there was the bright light that caused me to trip over a rock and break the camera. I hope that it's the battery. That light made me feel dizzy, kinda like time got away from me. It was only a second, yet my watch says I missed about twenty minutes. But I don't know," he said, uncertain how to explain it.

"I've got an extra battery over here if you want to test that out first," suggested Patti.

"Yeah, I'm hoping that's all it is," replied Parker.

She handed him a new battery pack, and as soon as he opened the door, removed the old battery, and inserted the new one, the camera returned to life. After the logo subsided and the camera roll images were visible, Parker breathed a sigh of relief, knowing the device didn't break. Good thing too, because that was an expense from his check he didn't need. Now it was time to check the footage.

Hopefully there is footage, he thought.

His expectations increased as the green video played the footage of filming the bend, then jerking the camera after picking up movement. He detected there was something in the film, even if it was bumpy from his running. Then he saw the footage of the camera leaving his hand, taking a short flight, and then coming to a hard crash on the ground. Luckily, when it landed, somewhat on its side, there was a portion of the screen not blocked by the grass that occupied the lower third of the frame.

"Hey guys? Check this out. What do you make of that?" Parker asked, with a puzzled look.

"It is something," Buck said, leaning in to get a closer look. "Can you zoom in?"

"Yeah, what is that?" added Jocasta. "It's a creature. But I don't know what kind of creature."

"Look, there are three of them!" said an excited Patti, pointing at the screen.

"They look about four feet tall if you use those trees down there as a comparison," said Parker.

"Smooth skin. No hair on it at all. Bipedal. Hard to see what color they are. Look kind of gray or green in this night vision."

"I remember catching a glimpse," said Parker. "Then when I was on the ground, I remember it had something and then…" his explanation drifted off.

A bright light flashed on across the monitor, showing everything as a ball of white for a second. Then the film returned to show the unidentified being were gone. One thing was clear in the video. That was the sound of groans as Parker returned to consciousness on the ground. The video then showed a black screen as the camera shut down after it reached its battery limit.

"Didn't they look... like ... frogs?" asked Patti

"Yeah, but I don't know of any bipedal frog that stands about four feet and looks to weigh a good seventy-five pounds," answered Buck.

"Maybe someone does," added Jocasta. "Maybe someone online. We should upload this video to the internet and see if anyone else has a clue."

CHAPTER 4

FACT OR FAKED

In the T.I.M.E. Agency's office at 603 Davis Street in Austin, Kareem, Jourdyn, and Tegan sat on a blue sectional with their morning coffee around a glass table, ready for the weekly team meeting. Carson walked into the room blowing cooler breath into his *I'm Not a Monster* coffee cup, sporting a crying image of the Loch Ness Monster. The faded jeans and the Austin Ice Bats t-shirt reflected it was Casual Friday. The dress code was casual on most days in the office unless a client had made an appointment.

"How's the hangover?" asked Kareem.

"Dude, I haven't felt like this in a long time," Carson said as he took a sip of the Major Gomez dark roast blend from Austin Roasting Company. "Mmm," he hummed, as he tasted the dark chocolate, smooth, smoky flavor of the coffee. "I need this kick to get me going this morning," he added as he pulled a chair out from the glass table and sat down, placing files on the table.

"Where's Ty?" asked Tegan.

"Right here," said a disembodied voice that located its body when Ty walked into the room from his office.

"Sorry, I was a little distracted checking out some videos," he said. "Matter of fact, there's a video you guys should check out. I've watched it a dozen times and can't figure it out," he said, placing his laptop on the table and turning it so everyone on the sectional could see it.

Carson scooted his chair to the side and handed Ty a coffee mug from the table. Ty clicked play on the video.

"What are we seeing here?" asked Carson. "Green, grainy night vision camera. Camera guy running. Slightly blurry." He paused his assessment and raised his head to ask, "Why are photos and videos of creatures always blurry? Chrissakes, it's the twenty-first century, people!" he exclaimed.

"Keep watching. The camera man thinks he sees something, but the camera doesn't pick it up," Ty said, pointing to the video.

"This video is bouncing too much to see. It's like the *Blair Witch*," Carson added. "Oh, the camera is in the air. He must have dropped it," Carson reacted as the video showed the camcorder hitting the ground and filming the corner of the yard. "That's coming out of someone's paycheck," replied Carson.

"The grass is high, but we get a good visual above the blade line," analyzed Kareem. He squinted at the screen, attempting to get a better look. "What are those?" he asked, seeing the three unknown figures in the moonlit corner.

"I'm not sure," Carson said, getting out of the chair and taking a knee near the laptop.

The video showed the unknown subjects walking around the grassy area, stopping to look at the cameraman lying on the ground, and then one raised what appeared to be a slender arm. Seconds later, a bright light emanated from an object in the subject's hand. The screen was a sea of white, then after returning to normal, the beings were gone, and then the camera went black.

"Looks like the battery died there," stated Tegan.

"Paranormal activity in the area, or an ill-timed dead battery?" asked Ty.

"What do you know about this video? Where was it shot?" Carson asked.

"Fairly new. Went viral in a couple two days. It's posted by a group called Porkopolis Paranormal Society and it's filmed in Loveland, Ohio," Ty told.

"Porkopolis?" asked Jourdyn.

"That's what they called Cincinnati back in the 1800s because it was the largest pork-producing city in the world," said Ty.

"Loveland… Loveland… where do I know that name from?" asked Carson.

Tegan hung her head upon hearing the name of the town. She drifted off into a daydream as she recalled the events in the below ground secret lab at Dream Draw. Carson noticed her reaction and remembered the stress and uncertainty she went through.

"The folders," said Kareem.

"The folders from the folders we pulled from that secret underground lab in Phoenix!" Carson remembered.

"Not *we*," said Tegan. "*I* found them." She remembered the frightening feeling of being beneath the dam, uncertain of what might lurk in the shadows. She remembered the tons of files, the unknown spells and chemicals, and the alien spaceship.

Can't forget that, she thought.

"Well… *we*. You and me," said Kareem. "I went too… later," he reminded.

"You're right. We did," Tegan said. "It's… I am still shaken up by what I saw down there. Especially the first time, when it was only me and whatever might be down there. I had to see a therapist for it. Still am," Tegan added.

"I thought you were the therapist?" replied Carson.

"Different kind of therapist. Hell, therapists might need therapy the most," she said. "We deal with a lot of things and have to compartmentalize it and move on."

"I did not know you were going through that," replied Ty.

"I deal with it my own way and move on. Whatcha gonna do?" she asked rhetorically. "Speaking of moving on, have you looked through those folders?" she asked Carson.

"Not a lot, no. I flipped through them and filed them for a time when we had some downtime, but that time hasn't come, apparently. I organized that drawer recently. I'm surprised the name didn't stick out to me better because of that," he admitted.

"I'll get the Loveland file," said Jourdyn as she got up and walked toward Carson's office. "This will be much easier when I finish loading the files onto a flash drive so you each can have one. Who knows what information is buried in those documents. Something helpful might stand out to you if you have time to review them in detail."

"You helped me when I needed it back when we first met," Carson said. "If there's anything you need or anything I can do, let me know."

"I'm okay. Sometimes things trigger those feelings. Hearing Loveland and remembering everything about what happened. One of the few files I got a glimpse of in the lab had the name Loveland. Remembering that must have done the trick. But I'm good now," she said.

Jourdyn returned with the folder and handed it to Carson.

"Thank you," he said as he opened it. "Let's see what's inside."

The folder was thin, containing only a few newspaper articles and a two-page summary of details from interviews, a recap of the older sightings, a couple of photos from investigations, and some physical description.

"Not a lot here to go on," said Carson. "I was expecting these folders to contain more valuable information," he replied.

"Roll that video back, can you?" he asked Ty. "Take us to where those three things appear near the end," requested Carson. "Check out those creatures on the video, and then look at this photo from the folder. They look similar, don't you think?" Carson said, as he passed a small black and white 4" x 5" photograph to Kareem.

"Both are difficult to see. The photo is small, and the video isn't in complete focus, but I agree they look similar," Kareem stated.

"What are they? Does it say in the reports?" asked Tegan.

"Yes, at least we have that information," Carson reviewed. The first report was an eyewitness account from the spring of 1955. A young traveling salesperson named Robert Hunnicutt was driving along Madeira-Loveland Pike near the Branch Hill area of Loveland, Ohio, where the report says he saw three strange, two-legged entities standing upright in the road. They appeared to be huddled together in a triangle formation. Stopping the vehicle, he pulled over to the side of the road and watched for approximately three minutes until the creatures noticed him.

"Did he get a good look at them?" asked Ty.

"It gives a description in this report," read Carson. "Human-like in appearance except for heads that looked like a frog. They had green skin, an enormous mouth, gigantic eyes, and a hairless body. He claims they had the smell of almonds and alfalfa, but from the reports, it doesn't look like he got out of the car nor was close enough to pick up a smell. He also claims they had a type of wand or a chain that gave off blue and white sparks like a Fourth of July sparkler," read Carson.

"Sparklers? We saw a bright light at the end of the video, and it looked like one creature was holding up something," remembered Tegan.

"What happened to the creatures in that encounter?" asked Ty.

"Looks like Hunnicutt had enough and feared the creatures, so he drove off," revealed Carson. "The reports suggest that Hunnicutt at some point lost consciousness, and he reported the sense of a loss of time. The notes here state those two states are thought to be connected," stated Carson.

"This report is from the police? Did they investigate the area?" asked Kareem.

"Yes, looks like Hunnicutt reported the incident to the Chief of Police, John Fritz. He went out to investigate the area... after Hunnicutt passed a field sobriety test in his office. Hunnicutt was a member of the Loveland Civil Defense, which was like a community preparedness group back then, and police believed him to be credible, but they found nothing," said Carson.

"Is there any more information in the folder? Asked Teagan.

"Not from that night, but there is another incident here. Looks like two months after Hunnicutt's sighting. Still in 1955. A young woman named Emily Mangone and her husband claimed their dogs were barking and woke them up. They turned on the lights and saw a three-foot tall creature covered in leaves and mud that ran off when the lights came on, but later returned when the lights were off again. It doesn't give a physical description except the height of the creature," stated Carson. "Another sighting in July 1955 came from a couple who lived in Loveland, but were driving to Florida. They saw the same creatures in Stockton, Georgia."

"So all three sightings are from 1955?" asked Ty.

"That's all the investigative info we have," he said, handing a couple of pages to Ty.

"That's a pretty intense story," said Kareem. "Even though we don't have a lot, that's a good tip to start us off."

Carson continued to flip through the pages in the file.

"Seems to have died down after those 1955 encounters, at least for a few years. Next story in here is from 1972. Oh, and this one is from a police officer," revealed Carson.

"A police officer in Loveland? That should be good evidence. What did he see?" asked Tegan.

"The report shows March 3, 1972, an officer Ray Shockey, Jr. driving Riverside Road at 1 a.m., and it says the road conditions were bad. It was March, and the weather was frigid and icy that night. He saw something in the bend in the road that he thought was an injured animal, so he slowed down to see what it was. He said it hunched down like a frog, but then it stood in a bipedal position. He got a good look at it because it was in the car's headlights," read Carson.

"What did he see?" asked Kareem.

"He gives the exact coordinates of the incident and described the creature as between fifty and seventy-five pounds, smooth leather-like skin with folds and bumpy texture, and hind legs that were longer than its front arms, allowing it to walk upright. He describes the head as like a frog. It looked at him for a moment, then turned and jumped over a guard rail before disappearing into the Little Miami River," continued Carson.

"That's a detailed report. Did the department follow up on it?" asked Ty.

"It says he filed the report with Officer Mark Matthews. Matthews and Shockey returned to the scene of the incident," added Carson.

"Did they find anything?" asked Tegan.

"Says they found some tracks where the creature he saw slid down toward the river. They found there were scratches on the guardrail in that exact location. They thought perhaps it was from the creature," revealed Carson.

"At least the other officer believed him," said Kareem.

"This is interesting," Carson said as he turned another page. "It doesn't say if Matthews believed his partner, but two weeks later Matthews himself drove along a road in Loveland on March 17, 1972, and thought he saw a dead animal in the road. He pulled over to see if he could move it, but when he got out of the vehicle, the creature stood up. The description here is like the others: three to four feet tall, smooth leather-like skin with bumps and folds, frog-like head, but this time it mentions having a tail. That's interesting because while the descriptions are similar, none of the others mention a tail," replied Carson.

"So two officers in the area reported a similar creature. You would think the police would pursue that with a larger investigation," added Ty.

"No, instead, those two officers received taunts and ridicule from fellow officers. So much so, they stopped talking about it and Matthews later recanted his story to say it was a giant lizard. Perhaps someone's pet iguana got too big, and they turned it loose," said Carson.

"That's not uncommon for people who see a cryptid or anything unusual to be harassed by others to where they stop talking about it," replied Tegan.

"Remember in San Antonio? Many people saw things but were afraid to come forward because of what they thought others would think. Having that town hall meeting and getting everyone in one room talking about it helped cut through that and allowed people to be honest with what they were seeing out there," replied Kareem.

"So those last two stories, if this is some kind of frog or lizard or even iguana, you said it was cold. Those are cold-blooded creatures. Since they don't create their own internal temperature and have to take on the temperature of their surroundings, they aren't about in the snow and icy weather," said Ty.

"Good point. The earlier stories were in May or later, but March would be cold. Some of the other reports in here are in warm weather, like July 2002. But the winter months are a strange occurrence," said Carson.

"There's some brief mention on a notebook page about Native American stories of the *Twightwee* tribe. They describe a river monster they called the *Shawnahooc*, and it guarded the shores of the Little Miami River to keep unwanted people away. Remember when we investigated Champ, and those sightings went back to Native American folklore as well," said Ty. "There is a word written in the margin on this page that says Hopkinsville, but no sign of how it relates."

"It's hard to see solid detail on this video you showed us, Ty, but from what we can see, it seems like a similar creature. The height is right, the skin looks hairless, and you can see some texture there, and they are bipedal. There are a couple of words jotted on the top of a page in the folder: *Ohio Frogmen* and *Loveland Frog*," said Carson.

"Although the description mentions the appearance of a frog, there are many knocks against it being a frog," said Ty.

"The cold weather is one knock against it and frogs are not bipedal," said Kareem.

"Holding an object in its front feet or arms isn't something a frog could do," added Tegan, as she shivered thinking about frogs.

"This video is gaining traction with thousands of views, and it's only been online a few days," said Ty.

"This story is intriguing. These paranormal guys picked footage of something, but who knows what?" said Kareem.

"Right. This paranormal group seems to know what they're doing in their field. Ty, you said they've been around a while and have a solid history of credibility. One thing I hate is the fact that people lump anything unexpected together. These guys don't know what they are seeing because they are ghost hunters," said Carson.

"And the cameraman biffed it on the rock," added Ty.

"Yes, that too. But they are not experts in cryptids. A ghost and a cryptid are both unknown to most people, but they are different fields. You can't expect the ghost hunter to know about the Loveland Frog because it also is an unknown or unusual creature," ranted Carson.

"As much as I hate to say it, there's only one way to get to the bottom of it," started Tegan.

"Jourdyn, see if you can get us a flight to Ohio!" interrupted Carson.

"Let's hope they are not frogs. I hate frogs," said Tega

CHAPTER 5

STRAPHANGER

Morning clouds gave way to afternoon rain, but Vivian Gregory was undeterred as she rode her bicycle along Central Parkway from downtown Cincinnati until it emerged north of the Western Hills Viaduct. The rain was a light shower, but the Columbia hooded rain jacket kept her dry. She squinted as she continued her ride along Central until she saw the Plan–Build–Live mural ahead. There, she turned left onto a blacktop road that turned toward I-75, but served as an access road toward her destination. Graffiti covered cement on the left side while cars sped along the heavily trafficked highway on her right. The road was below Central Parkway and above the interstate, yet most people drove past this site without ever noticing. Soon she reached her goal. It was a large gray door with a metal gate resting on its top.

As she approached the metal doors, she found the padlock picked and fallen to the ground. The door was heavy, but she dragged it enough to open it wider. Slipping through the door, she emerged into an interior draped in total darkness. Although she pulled the door open a few feet, it was wide enough for her to slip into the opening. At five-foot-three and one-hundred-fifteen pounds, the young urban explorer didn't need a wide opening.

This was the main entrance to the abandoned Cincinnati subway, America's largest unused subway system. Construction began in 1920 and ran for five years until the original six million dollars budget ran dry. Because of rising costs and inflation, the city put the project on a temporary hold. The start of the Great Depression caused it to become a permanent hold, with only two miles of the underground system completed.

She knew the underground system was unsafe and monitored by Cincinnati police, but that was part of the thrill for her as she enjoyed exploring abandoned man-made ruins and hidden structures long forgotten by the modern world. Her interest in historical documentation and photography served as her primary motivation for the hobby. The air inside was damp and musty. She looked around the large open area to get a sense of her surroundings. The few rays of late that broke through into the underground chamber were not enough to light the way. She kneeled and removed her backpack, unzipped it, and removed a headlamp. She turned on the lamp and attached it. The light's illumination lit up her immediate area and gave her a better look at her surroundings. Next, she removed an old paper map of the subway system and her digital camera to take pictures of her adventurous find.

She found herself in a large cement tunnel with a black dirt floor and reinforced concrete walls covered with graffiti. Based on how easy it was to enter, she expected that she wasn't alone. She heard stories of homelessness and illegal activities rumored to take place in the tunnel, and while she was undeterred, it didn't mean she wouldn't keep her guard up.

As she walked down the tunnel, she noticed a cement wall with several openings separating the second line of the subway. She stepped through the opening and discovered more graffiti on the opposite walls and metal supports holding the structure in place. The parallel tubes of the subway looked about fifteen feet high and maybe thirteen feet wide. Further inside, the dirt floor turned to cement and wooden runners where the rails were to have attached. The echoes increased as she disappeared deeper into the dark underground tunnel. She whistled and listened to the echo bounce off the walls before she continued her journey into the unknown. For most of the tunnel, she knew the two lines remained separated, except for a few portals where it opened into a single room.

Exploring the tunnel, she found some evidence of modern usage, including city water lines and fiber optics conduits, but most of the tunnel remained as it was over a hundred years ago. Deeper into the tunnel, every sound reverberated throughout the walls, making it difficult to distinguish its origin or location. She heard drips she thought sounded like the water hitting something other than a puddle. The sounds of trucks driving on the road above amplified, creating an eerie sound that caused her to slow her advancement. The acoustics of the tunnel drew her toward another opening, where she discovered the sound generated by dripping water hitting a plastic tarp over the water main piping.

After thirty minutes of walking deeper into the tunnel, she felt the air, while still stuffy, opened as she found her way to a station entrance. She stood on the floor of the tunnel where the tracks would be in an operational subway. A small wooden ladder reached from the ground to the three-hundred-foot-long platform a few feet above. This would have been a busy station with passengers waiting for the next oncoming train. She found another set of wooden steps on her right. Her footsteps echoed throughout the tunnel with each step as she reached the top and peered into what appeared to be the abyss of the opposite side. This led to the opposite platform where the subway would have gone up to the street.

She passed a large open room that was empty except for trash and graffiti on the walls. Passing the room, a large cement staircase led to the surface where passengers would have entered and exited, but now a large metal grate, locked from above, covered it. The closed grate prevented any light from reaching into the tunnel. She stopped and took photos of the area behind her.

"One station down, three more to go," she said aloud to herself.

At least, she hoped it was to herself.

Deeper still, she found what appeared to be an access shaft, but they bricked it off. She snapped a few photos as the sound of the shutter echoed in the tunnel. Again, she heard cars and what appeared to be people talking above her. Her headlamp was at full power, but the length of the tunnel prevented her from seeing any end in sight. She stopped when she reached station number two, the Linn Street Station, but found it was sealed off, filled in with a cement and cinder block wall that covered the entire length of the platform. One third of the way through the subway system, she had been underground for over an hour and only reached two of the four stations. She paused, wondering if she should continue, knowing that each addition step deeper inside would mean that many steps she would have to take to return to the surface where she began this journey.

She looked down at her map. The headlamp shining on its surface, showing her current location and how much of the tunnel remained ahead. She knew the third station contained a fallout shelter and the last station had a platform in the middle of the tunnel. She looked at the map, and then scanned her surroundings to consider her options. The idea of turning back still stayed in her mind, but the opportunity to explore this site had been on her local urban explorer bucket list for a long time. She returned the map to the backpack and continued.

She arrived at the Liberty Street Station, one of the more interesting points along the subway system because of its repurposing in the 1960s as a fallout station. A metal ladder allowed her access to the platform, where a lighting system was still in place but non-operational. At the top of the platform, a chain-link fence ran the length of the platform opening. Similar to what she observed in the early sections of the subway, the interior walls and cement seating were covered in graffiti on all sides. She walked along the platform and located an opening into a large hallway that continued several hundred feet to another opening that served as an entrance or exit to the street above. Another large metal grail closed off the street entrance. A grail she had seen from above at the intersection of Liberty and Central.

Walking through the fallout shelter, she found openings in several other rooms. Her research revealed during the fallout shelter's operational days, the city stocked many of the rooms with food and allowed people to remain underground for a long period. Today there was no food and scatter littler occupied many of the rooms with trash while the air hung thick with dust. One shortcoming of the shelter was its size. It was much too small to provide safety to many people, even the smaller population Cincinnati had back in the Sixties.

As she walked through the rooms with her headlight illuminating things that hadn't seen light in years, she found some rooms still had beds. They were metal frames with metal springs, like what one might find in a prison. She imagined being limited to this fabricated underground cavern would feel like a prison, even after a couple of days, to people who would have sought shelter.

Around a sharp corner, almost a full ninety-degree curve underneath Plum Street, the wall opened taller and cement passages forked off in multiple directions. Staying with the main tunnel, she reached the opening for the largest station, the Race Street Station, beneath downtown Cincinnati.

It was commodious compared to the prior tunnels and stations on the early leg of the journey. Here the line split into three openings: a center platform station and a line on either side. Another sealed off staircase prevented her access to the street surface. Another set of stairs descended into the darkness. She took them, but stopped after seeing they too ended in a dead end.

Considering her options, she noticed two additional sets of stairs descended on each side of the tunnel. A cool breeze invited her to explore one of the side steps, but it ended at a cement wall, forcing her to retreat. With no workable stairs to exit the platform, she sat on the edge and dropped to the floor below.

The fall wasn't too far. Maybe four feet, but the impact of hitting the ground caused a large amount of dust to fly and the thud from her boots hitting the ground to fill the air and bounce off the walls. It surprised her that after exploring for over two and a half hours, she had not yet reached the end. Soon she discovered each of the tunnels had been closed off, ending in brick walls, forcing her to retreat. Her light shone on a large metal pipe, she realized must go somewhere. She followed it as it disappeared into the darkness on the other side of the wall from her initial entrance. Her headlamp shined ahead, showing the path covered by water. With limited options, she forged ahead, her feet splashed in the water even though she took slow, deliberate steps. The water proved to be shallower than she thought, perhaps only three or four inches deep in that area.

As she continued, her footsteps echoed louder, even though the tunnel walls were not as high as the platform entrance. Trying not to splash, she continued plodding through the tunnel, trying to push her feet instead of step, until she once again reached dry land.

She continued along the tunnel, following the large water pipe running through that portion of the room, only to once again discover the end of the tunnel blocked off once again, forcing her to return the way she came.

Vivian looked at her watch and it shocked her to see it had been four hours since she arrived. The lack of airflow made it uncomfortable, and the time was getting late. She didn't want to be stuck there after nightfall.

She imagined what visitors and activities might happen there at night, and she decided it was time to go back. Soon it would get dark on the surface above, and from the echoing sounds, the rain was harder now than when she first entered. She was excited to reach the end of the subway and knew that the return to the surface would not take as long as it took her to reach the end. 56

She wasn't surveying the environment on the way back as she did to get there, but there were still a lot of photos she planned on taking. She knew the way back was a straight path, the same way she came in. Not much over two miles, even at a standard pace, she should reach the entrance in about thirty minutes.

With each push of the shutter, the camera made a shickt sound followed by a flash of light that illuminated the tunnel a short distance. Not enough to see deep into the darkness, but enough to light the immediate area around her. Satisfied with her photos in this area, she continued her journey back to the surface.

Ahead, at least she thought it was coming from ahead. She heard a sound that she recalled being dripping water hitting the plastic tarp covering the water main inbound tube piping. She knew she was back to the outbound platform near Brighton Station and close to the beginning portal entrance by

Hopple Street. Another noise echoed throughout the tunnel, but this one didn't sound like water. It sounded like shuffling on gravel, which was not something she heard in the area when she passed it hours ago. The bouncing of the echoed sound made it difficult for her to identify the source's origin. She stopped and snapped her head over her shoulder, but all she saw was the short range of her headlamp followed by what appeared to be infinite darkness. She raised her camera and aimlessly snapped a few photos in the general direction, but with a maximum range of fifteen to twenty feet, the flash did not provide any answers. She dismissed the odd noise and continued toward the tunnel entrance. She paused, seeing a portal to a side room that she hadn't noticed when she arrived.

Secluded behind a bend in the tunnel, it wasn't noticeable coming from the other direction, but headed back she could see it jutted off into a lengthy hallway on the inbound side of the Brighton's Corner station platform. She reached into her backpack and again pulled out the map, noticing a hallway shown on the plans leading to a fifteen by fifteen square-foot bathroom. There were no bathrooms on the outbound side at Brighton's Corner. With the unique discovery and her current location near the subway entrance, she decided she had a few minutes to explore this new underground route.

Down the hallway behind the platform, she located additional small rooms that lead to larger storage areas where attendants would have performed maintenance duties. The sounds were louder as she walked further from the track and into the station's interior. As she turned her head while walking past one of the empty, open rooms, she thought she glimpsed eye shine as her headlamp reflected a yellowish color in the darkness.

She stopped and took a couple of steps back to get a good look into the room. She squinted her eyes and tried to identify what appeared to be silhouettes inside. Because of the eye shine, she theorized the source was an animal, not a human. She knew tapetum lucifum gave nocturnal carnivores superior night vision, but humans lacked it. She raised her camera and held down the shutter, snapping multiple photos, causing the flash to repeat, and light up the small room.

She strained her eyes again, thinking she could make out three distinct objects in the room. The flashing of the camera caused them to notice her as well. She stared, frozen and uncertain what she was seeing. The objects were not debris or bags of garbage, but appeared to resemble frogs, but unlike frogs, they were standing on two feet and looked to be about four feet tall. Their hairless features also suggested a creature more amphibian than a mammal.

Whatever it was, she knew she had seen nothing like it before and a frigid chill ran down her spine, alerting her to potential danger. Turning to flee, she reached back and snapped additional photos as she started running back toward the platform where she perceived safety to be a short distance away.

As she passed the platform, she continued toward the tunnel's entrance. The stuffiness of the tunnel and the time spent underground made it difficult to breathe, causing her to slow down to a slow job. She paused to catch her breath, but as she turned to look over her shoulder, she saw the creatures lumbering toward her.

While it shocked her to see them running after her, she stood aghast, watching after they dropped into a frog-like position and continued the chase. Realizing she had no time to waste, she again started running, and she didn't stop running until she reached the platform, then once again jumped down to the ground below.

Now she didn't worry about the sound she would make jumping to the floor below or if there were other humans in the tunnel. She knew something was there but wasn't sure what it was, and she would not stick around to find out.

Given the creatures' pursuit of her, she didn't think they were friendly. She moved rapidly, slowing down only to give another cursory glance over her shoulder to confirm they were still giving chase.

She reached the Hopple Street tunnel entrance and squeezed through the door into the nighttime air. It was still raining outside, but it didn't deter her from straining to push the door closed.

She looked around on the ground and found the padlock laying in a puddle close to her feet. She snatched the lock from the puddle and clumsily forced it into the door's latch, closing it and locking whatever those creatures were inside the dark tunnel. Exhausted, she slumped to the wet ground and leaned against the secured door. A loud thump on the other side signaled her pursuers had reached the portal.

A loud thump banged against the door, sounding as if the creatures were ramming themselves against the door, attempting to break out. She knew she couldn't stay long. She didn't know if they could find their way out of the portal, but she would not wait to find out. Picking herself up from against the door, she ran wearily to her bike, mounting it, and peddled up Hopple Street, back to Central, and toward downtown.

Her heart pounded against her chest harder than the creatures rammed against the door. She made her escape, knowing the heightened adrenaline would not permit her to sleep that night.

CHAPTER 6

PORTAL TO HELL

A passenger service agent walked over to prop the door at Cincinnati/Northern Kentucky International Airport's Gate B18 open with a rubber door jamb. Minutes later, passengers disembarked from the plane and passed through the waiting area. Ty was the first of the T.I.M.E. Agency team to emerge, followed by Tegan, Kareem, and Carson bringing up the rear. As they passed through the waiting area, Ty attempted to locate the arrivals board to see which carousel they would pick up luggage.

They walked through Terminal B and located the escalator past the Brooks Brothers and SPANX stores. Getting on the escalator to head to baggage claim and the ground transportation tunnel, overhead announcements provided safety updates from TSA, followed by a welcome to Cincinnati message. Ty listened for a moment.

"Is that…" Ty asked.

"I believe that's the voice of the Reds, Marty Brennaman," replied Carson.

"I like it," Ty added. "I don't like those cold, industrialized messages heard in airports. Marty's voice gives an immediate sense of local culture and a feel of the community."

"Growing up, I listened to the Red's broadcast. Marty and Joe Nuxhall were as much a part of the history and tradition of the Reds and the players themselves," replied Carson.

"And, we've got free Wi-Fi," discovered Kareem.

The flow of the airport was smooth for passengers to find their way around a location that might be new to them.

"Look at that large wooly mammoth," said Tegan, pointing ahead.

"That's an unexpected and hidden creature," said Kareem. "We should get a Welcome to Cincinnati selfie with it," he suggested.

The gang lined up for a few quick snapshots before continuing their journey downstairs. On the lower level of the terminal, all passengers walked past the convenient meeting area to greet arriving family and friends. In baggage claim, the group awaited their luggage, and the chance to hit the streets of Northern Kentucky.

"You guys want to fish out the luggage while I secure the rental car?" asked Carson.

"Works for me," replied Ty.

Carson clicked the Jeep Compass's unlock button, while Kareem and Ty loaded everything in the back using Ty's exceptional spatial reasoning skills.

"Thinking back to the Porkopolis Paranormal team specializing in ghosts, but running into a cryptid, we should check out a place known for paranormal activity while we are here," Carson suggested.

"I'm down. I've always wanted to go on a ghost hunt," replied Ty.

"Anything in mind?" asked Tegan

"Indeed, I do!" answered Carson. "The Cincinnati airport is in northern Kentucky, and there's a place I have wanted to visit for a long time. It's on the way to our hotel in Cincinnati."

"What is it?" asked Kareem.

"Bobby Mackey's Music World in Wilder, Kentucky," responded Carson.

"I've seen that place on *Ghost Adventures* twice," replied Tegan. "Spooky as hell!"

"It has a long history with a lot of mysterious and unusual happenings," said Kareem. "I've also seen those episodes, and I agree with Tegan!"

"You should be used to that now," answered Carson. "This is a different field, but one no more unusual than what we do. Think of the adventure," he enticed.

"Many believe Bobby Mackey's to be one of the most haunted locations in America," said Ty. "If we are going to go on a ghost hunt, might as well be one of the best."

"If we are doing our own investigation a few miles away, how *can* we miss one of the best locations of paranormal evidence? I mean, we're here, right?" replied Carson

Twenty minutes later, the group pulled into the crumbled blacktop parking lot of the former slaughterhouse. They parked at the edge of the road in a near deserted, bumpy parking lot. The large white building sat next to a quiet railroad track. Red lettering read *Bobby Mackey's* in the far-right corner of the building.

"This is the place," Carson said, shaking his hands on the steering wheel, while the others looked at the building and reacted to cold chills running up their spines from its mere presence. They sensed the energy of the property differed from the surrounding area. A dark energy grew in intensity as they began walking closer to the entrance. Pausing before opening the door, Carson turned and looked at his friends. "We ready to do this?" he asked.

"As ready as I'll ever be," replied Kareem. "But first, let's get a group selfie of the outside of the building for the T.I.M.E. scrapbook."

Inside they found Kaden McDaniel, a young man spending his third-year leading ghost tours at Bobby Mackey's, standing near a podium.

"Good afternoon," Kaden said with a welcoming smile. "Here for the tour?"

"Yes, we're in the area and this is a place I've wanted to check out for a long time," responded Carson.

"Great. We go in groups of six or eight, but we'll give it a few more minutes, and if no one else shows up, then it's only us. Ok?" he asked.

"Are we using any equipment?" asked Kareem.

"Your admission price includes the use of equipment. We have several flashlights or headlamps and whichever you prefer - thermal cameras, a KII EMF detector, a digital audio recorder, and an SB-7 spirit box," detailed Kaden.

After ten minutes, no one else showed up for the tour. Kaden looked down at his watch and up at the group.

"Well, let's get started," he said as he distributed various paranormal equipment to the group. Each member of the group received a headlamp; Kareem also received a digital recorder, Ty a full spectrum camera, Tegan a spirit box, and Carson a KII meter.

Even though the group had been on multiple cryptid investigations, each investigator felt a sense of nervousness at being in a location with such a reputation. The feeling intensified as Kaden began the tour.

"Those paranormal investigators expected to see ghosts but stumbled upon that cryptid. We do not know what to expect with this investigation," said Carson.

"Hopefully, we don't stumble on to any ghosts," replied Tegan. "I'm cool with most animals because we can see them. But I don't want to experience an unseen ghost."

"Or demons," Kareem interjected.

As Kaden led the way into the upstairs main area, a feeling of dark energy seemed to have dissipated. It felt more energetic and positive, likely from the many nights of high energy from the dancing, good live music, and the joviality of a dive bar people come to have a good time. While many experienced good times at the bar, Carson also sensed some feeling of depression and melancholy walking through the panel-covered walks and looking at the bar, pool tables, and even a mechanical bull. He felt a heaviness that affected his emotions. It reminded him of his days drinking alone in Giddy Ups back in Austin. He knew the feelings of those who were going through a tough time and wasting their days and nights in a local watering hole.

He mentally transported back to those days. He could visualize himself running his finger around the rim of a cold glass of Lone Star, searching its depths for answers before grabbing the handle and chugging its contents. Could those similar local patrons of the past contribute to the sense of negativity and depression that Carson felt entering the old honky-tonk?

Maybe the others in the group didn't notice that dark energy because they have not lived within its icy grasp as Carson had. They seemed to pick up more on the radiant energy that overcame and attempted to suppress the hopelessness. Even after a positive couple of years, Carson could still occasionally feel its cold pull, wanting to return and take over his life. He lingered in thought for a moment longer.

"Hey, you coming?" asked Ty as he noticed Carson had fallen behind.

A quick shake of his head after Ty's words and Carson snapped back to the present.

"Yeah, I'm taking in the scenery," Carson said, giving a slow jog to catch up to his friend.

"The downstairs area is the basement. That's where most of the action takes place. But let's save that for later," Kaden said as he turned toward a wooden staircase heading up. "Carl's room is upstairs," Kaden announced.

"Carl Lawson?" asked Ty.

"Yes, one of our former employees," replied Kaden.

"The possessed one?" asked Kareem.

"He became possessed not only while working here, but he also lived here at Bobby Mackey's," Kaden responded.

The wooden handrail wobbled as they held onto it while ascending the stairs, rising higher up the makeshift pine-paneled walls. No matter how careful their step, the staircase omitted a loud creak beneath every footstep.

"Here on the staircase," Tegan began before pausing and drawing in a deep inhale, "Is that... rose? I think I smell something like a rose perfume right here. Something I didn't smell in the other room," she asked.

Kaden stopped and turned to face the group.

"Rose? Back in the 1950s, this place was a nightclub called The Latin Quarter, and was the most popular bar in the area. The owner was successful and one of his daughters, Johanna Jewels, was a popular dancer there. She caught the eye of a singer, Robert, who played at the Latin Quarter. Upon hearing that his daughter became pregnant by the singer, Johanna's father had him killed. Johanna was so devastated, she retaliated against her father, killing him, and then later taking her own life. They said she wore rose-scented perfume, and many who claimed to feel her presence first notice the scent of rose in the air," Kaden reported.

The cryptid investigators gaped at each other upon hearing the tale. A loud audible *creek* occurred near the base of the stairs causing the team to scamper up the stairs again, realizing they were the only ones in the building and they each had been standing still. Kaden swung open the pine door once the group reached the platform at the top of the stairs.

"After you," he said.

"This is where Carl stayed," Kaden stated.

The group stepped in and scanned the area. It was now a wide-open room with framing where a wall used to be. The kitchen was still intact in the back of the room, and off to the right behind an exposed sheet metal wall, the bathroom.

"It's a little heavier in here," said Ty, walking further into the room. "Can you feel it?"

"Yeah, I feel it too," confessed Kareem. "Maybe I should try the digital recorder?"

"After that, let's try the spirit box," added Tegan. "I've always wanted to use one!"

The group ambled around the room, littered with debris, while Kareem panned the area with the digital recording. Kaden gave them time to explore and attempt to catch evidence of the afterlife.

"Is anyone here with us?" Kareem asked. "Carl? Are you here? Johanna? Were you on the stairs with us? We thought we smelled your perfume," Kareem concluded.

After a couple of minutes, he stopped and rewound the tape.

"Let's see if we caught something," Kareem said in a more optimistic and upbeat tone.

He pressed play on the recorder and listened for any signs of a disembodied reply. However, they heard none. The only sound came from him asking questions and an occasional reaction from the wooden floor when someone from the group took a step.

"Damn… I'm a little disappointed," Kareem said dejectedly.

"Let's see what the spirit box can do," replied an eager Tegan.

She turned the device on, and the steady heavy static of white noise played as the machine swept through radio channels at different scanning speeds. Tegan cupped the device as she had seen others do on television when using a similar device.

"Johanna? Robert? Are you here? Are you looking for Johanna?" she asked. "How did you die? Was Johanna's dad responsible for your death?" she said as she removed her hand from the top of the device and listened to the static response.

A male voice replied, *Mob*.

"Were you killed by the mob?" asked Tegan, but the device returned to only a steady stream of static.

"Besides dancing, movies, and shows here at the Latin Quarters, there was also a lot of gambling," replied Kaden. "They alleged that Johanna's father was involved with criminal activity, and he used those connections to have Robert killed," he concluded.

"That sounds horrible," replied Carson.

"She scribed a poem to Robert on the wall that also served as a suicide note. When she killed herself in the basement, she was five months pregnant," added Kaden.

"Did the Latin Quarter close after her death?" asked Ty.

"It closed in 1961 after the sheriff cracked down on organized crime. It remained closed until it reopened in 1970 as the Hard Rock Cafe - no relation to the chain that exists today," added Kaden. "But eventually that too closed down. The Hard Rock was open seven years but closed because of the number of shootings that took place here. Then one year later, Bobby Mackey's Music World opened and has been here ever since," he finished.

"Sounds like quite a dark history," added Carson.

"There's more. Prior to the Latin Quarter, from 1930 to 1950, it was Buck Brady's Primrose Club, a local casino. According to local lore, that's when the organized crime moved in. It closed and later reopened as the Latin Quarter. In the 1920s it was the Bluegrass Inn," told Kaden.

"So it's been a nightclub, in some form, since 1920?" asked Ty.

"Yes, there have been a few empty years, but it has often been an active night club right here beside the railroad tracks,"

Kaden responded. "They built it in 1850 as a slaughterhouse and it operated until 1890."

"Slaughterhouse?" asked Tegan.

"Yes, cows would arrive right there on the train. The basement was used to slaughter the cattle and a tunnel in the basement used to channel the drained blood from the slaughterhouse into the nearby Licking River," Kaden answered.

"A tunnel from the basement to the river," repeated Kareem.

"That's what Bobby says. Others say that's a well that is the portal to hell," Kaden replied.

"The portal to hell! Yes, that's what I heard. That's where they dumped the girl's body?" asked Carson.

"Yes, Pearl Bryan. Legend says that in 1886, Scott Jackson and Alonzo Walling murdered Pearl and threw her severed head down the well. But they did not find it," added Kaden.

"That was the blood sacrifice to the devil they talk about?" asked Carson.

"That's the story. For years they rumored the slaughterhouse was a site where occultists performed rituals and could hide remains of small animals sacrificed during the ceremonies," Kaden said.

"Once it opened as Bobby Mackey's, how did it turn from a happy night club to one of the most haunted places in the country?" asked Ty.

"I don't know how it turned," stated Carson. "Sounds like there was a lot of dark energy here, maybe from the slaughterhouse, maybe from the occult ceremonies, but Kaden mentioned a long history of violence, including suicides, shootings, and killings. Maybe this place and the dark energy here drove those people to violence. One business after another came and went because of the violence and energy of the building," he added.

"If that well is a tunnel to the river, that could be why they never found Pearl's head," theorized Kareem.

"The ghosts appeared soon after Bobby Mackey's opened. Not only did they find the poem to Robert, but also Carl Lawson found a diary of Johanna's. He was the first employee hired by Bobby, and he was the first person to report hauntings," stated Kaden.

"It seems to have more than its share of violence and strange happenings," observed Ty.

"Let's head back out to the parking lot and we will check out the basement, if that's okay with everyone?"

"We've come this far." Kareem's voice trailed off as they walked to the back of the building and opened the basement door.

"It feels heavy again out here," said Carson.

"That's what we noticed when we got here. Even before we entered the building," said Ty.

"Probably energy emanating from the basement," replied Kaden.

"The basement? That's what I saw on the ghost shows," answered Carson.

Kaden said, "We have to go back outside and into the parking lot to get to the basement through the door at the back of the building… and that is where the energy intensifies."

"Even more? I'm already feeling it," stated Carson.

As Kaden described, the dreadful, negative energy increased downstairs. The change was detectable as soon as the group entered the doorway into the dark room, lit by red-bulb lamps that provided a higher level of eeriness.

"Damn, this is creepy!" said Tegan.

"I'd describe it as… evil," suggested Ty.

The basement was large, cluttered with tools, wood, ladders, and general maintenance tools and supplies needed to maintain the property.

"I'm going to snap photos on this full spectrum camera," said Ty.

"Good idea. You never know what we might find right here," replied Carson as he turned on the KII meter.

Exploring the basement, the group made their way into a back room with stairs leading to nowhere and a makeshift wooden fence made from 2" x 4" boards that kept visitors out of the well.

The area behind the fence had no light, only dirt, an exposed floor, and brick walls with peeling paint. They approached the fence with Ty randomly shooting photos in succession, before stopping near the rail overlooking the abyss of the well. Darkness prevented them from seeing too far into the pit below.

"This is the portal to hell?" asked Ty.

"Yes, this is it," replied Kaden.

Carson leaned over the rail and peered down into the opening, but even with his headlamp, he could only see a few feet. "Looks like it could descend to hell," he observed.

Tegan moved closer to the opening before turning on the spirit box, hoping to hear from Pearl, Scott, or Alonzo. The spirit box came to life once again with the sound of static white noise.

The camera's images illuminated the area in a bright purple hue. Snapping photo after photo, the images revealed nothing out of the ordinary except one showing a black shadow in the corner behind the well.

"What is that?" exclaimed Ty as he pointed at the display screen.

"I don't know, but it's not in any of the other photos, even though I took them in succession," observed Carson.

Scanning the area behind the wooden fence, Carson picked up some movement on the KII. Kareem panned the area with the thermal, seeing dark blue from the cold coming from the well's opening.

"My name is Kareem. Is anybody in here with us?" he asked into the digital recorder. "We came from Texas and would like to meet you," he continued.

Kareem pushed stop, then rewind on the device before pressing play as the group listened. It shocked them to hear a voice over Kareem's voice, but the words were undistinguishable.

"What was that?" asked Carson. "Try it again."

Tegan walked off to a side room that was only about eight feet square. It had an open door and inside, two chairs. She entered and sat on one chair, hoping the enclosed room would aid in her spirit box session. She thought perhaps that sitting in the chair might cause the spirits to react.

"Wait, do you hear that?" asked Ty from the main room. "There's someone walking down here."

"I hear footsteps," replied Kareem.

"Hello?" called out Ty. He waited a moment before repeating the question.

"I feel like something is here," said Carson, despite no response received from Ty's question.

"Did you kill Pearl?" Tegan asked from the small room as the spirit box continued running. "Is her head at the bottom of that well?" she asked.

The static from the spirit box continued until a man's voice broke the silence.

"It is."

"Guys!" she whispered, causing Kareem to leap to the open doorway.

"Did you pick up something?" he asked.

"Yes, a voice. Let's try again," she said.

The static returned, and soon it broke up again by the apparent sound of an animal.

"Did you hear that?" asked Kareem. "Sounded like a dark bark."

"I heard something, but we're near the back door. Maybe it's a dog outside?" she asked.

"Could be, but it sounded like it was coming from the speaker," he said.

After no more voices, the two gave up.

"Let's rejoin the others," Tegan suggested.

Ty and Carson continued to investigate the area around the well but also were lacking any additional evidence.

"That was creepy," said Kareem. "Tegan picked up a man's voice, and I swear we heard a dog come through the speaker box."

"That's not surprising," replied Kaden. "We have had reports of a dog spirit here in the basement."

"Maybe it was Carl's dog?" asked Kareem.

"Might be," replied Kaden. "Carl was the property's handy man and spent a lot of time here in the basement to keep the place in repair," added Kaden.

"You said Carl found Johanna's dairy and was the first to see ghosts," began Ty.

"That's correct, and many other strange occurrences like locked doors opening by themselves, lights flickering, and the jukebox playing on its own - including songs that weren't even on the jukebox," replied Kaden.

"And he became possessed?" asked Tegan.

"That's right. They say multiple demons attacked him before the devil eventually possessed him himself," stated Kaden.

"And there was an exorcism conducted on him?" asked Carson.

"Correct. You may have seen the video on television," replied Kaden. "The exorcism took place on August 8, 1991, and lasted over six hours."

"Six hours? That's crazy! Where was it conducted?" asked Kareem.

"Right upstairs in his apartment," said Kaden. "It seems to be successful initially. For a while, everything was quiet, but things started to pick up again and strange occurrences started happening at the club. It increased over the next few years until he died January 27, 2012, at the age of fifty-three," reported Kaden.

"Wow, I bet that was some experience. I only know of exorcisms from the movies," stated Tegan. "Must have been painful,. At least he's at rest now."

"Is he?" asked Kaden. "Some say they still hear him throughout the building," he said, with a turn back toward the door. "And that's the end of the tour. Shall we?" he said, extending a hand towards the exit.

The group walked back to the front of the building with more chills and questions than they started with.

"If you don't mind, can you follow me up to the equipment room to return the devices?" asked Kaden. "It helps speed up the closing process."

"We don't mind. I enjoyed it. It must be so fascinating to work here," said Carson.

"Mostly, yeah. Still getting used to the unexplained events here, ya know? I've seen things I never imagined being here," Kaden said as he opened the storage closet, to allow the group to return the items to their place. "We know how you feel," replied Tegan.

Closing the door, the group walked across the floor toward the entrance of Bobby Mackey's. As they pushed open the door to leave, on the opposite side of the room a pint glass slid unseen across the length of the bar, crashing to the ground mere seconds after the bar door closed shut.

Rhinegeist Brewery is a Cincinnati favorite, not to mention one of the largest breweries in the state of Ohio by sales volume and a top thirty independent craft brewery in the country. Walking inside, it surprised the group with its size. Over twenty-five-thousand-square-feet with an expansive open tap room. As expected, people packed the bar, enjoying the evening after a long day of work.

Kareem pulled up the website from his phone as they waited, searching for a table.

"Clever," he said. "The brewery is in a suburb called Over-the-Rhine, and the name Rhinegeist is German for *Ghost of the Rhein*," Kareem read.

"I think I speak for everyone when I saw I think we've had enough ghosts for one night," said Ty.

"Well, we didn't *see* one, although we got some evidence," started Carson. "And besides, I think we will all love the ghosts this place offers."

They found seating at one of the many wooden picnic tables in the main room as the music overhead played late sixties/seventies local Cincinnati band, Bo Donaldson and The Heywoods' *Billy Don't be a Hero*.

"We may not have come face to face with anything at Bobby Mackey's, but the feelings of dread, evil, and creepiness were there," said Ty. "And I could use a drink to help calm those feelings."

"Here are a few menus for you. My name is Dahlia and I'll be your server tonight. The draft menu is on there, as well as a few vintage bottles we have in stock, or you can always use the updated menu on Untappd," Dahlia said. "I'll come back with some waters and give you a couple minutes to look the menu over."

Kareem continued to review the web page for details on the brewery. "Origins are always cool stories," said Kareem. "So this brewery occupies the same site as an old Christian Moerlein Brewing Company that dated back to 1853. It closed because of Prohibition in 1919 before opening up later in the 1980s as the Hudepohl Brewing Company."

"If you think about it, that's a pioneer of craft beer. I remember them before they later became Hudepohl-Schoenling Brewing. Their focus was on building a better beer and that's the premise behind craft today," replied Ty.

"I remember them mentioned on the radio during those Cincinnati Reds or Bengal games I used to pick up on the radio as a teenager. One of their popular brands was Hudy Delight, I think it was," Carson recalled.

"Yeah, I believe you're right," said Ty. "That was a light beer introduced a couple of years after Miller Lite introduced a successful light beer to the country."

"Now it's resurrected under the old label, and sold at the Christian Moerlein Lager House here in town," said Kareem.

Carson's phone vibrated with a text from the home office. "It's Jourdyn," he read. "She said she has us booked to meet up with Parker Hickman and Buck Cane of the Porkopolis Paranormal Society tomorrow at a place called Listermann Brewing Company," read Carson.

"That's cool. I'm glad we can meet with the authors of that viral video. With that set, let's chill and find a place around here tonight. We can meet up with those guys tomorrow and see where we can get with learning more about the creatures in that video," suggested Ty.

Dahlia returned to the table, ready to take their order. Tegan ordered the Peach Dodo Gose, Carson the Truth American IPA, a Hustle Rye Pale Ale for Ty, and Kareem ordered the Saber Tooth Tiger Imperial IPA.

"Time to unwind. What a night it has been. I've always wanted to explore Bobby Mackey's, and we got to check it off the list, have a little fun exploring a local landmark, and we got some unexplained evidence," remembered Carson. "And this Truth IPA is another great surprise. This is one beer that put this brewery on the map. It's always highly rated and one that is not only putting this Over-the-Rhine area back on the brewing map, but the Cincinnati market."

"I love sour beers and this Peach Dodo is what I needed after Bobby Mackey's. A nice little kick with a tart initial taste, combined with enough salt and a peach taste that is present but not overpowering," analyzed Tegan.

"I'm getting some peach in this Saber Tooth as well. Along with some papaya and maybe mango. It's nice and smooth, almost like a hazy IPA. With a name like Sabre Tooth, I was expecting something harsher and fiercer, but it's soft and crushable," added Kareem.

"These guys do a great job to soften the taste of the beer. This one, too, is subtle. It has a detectable rye, but not overpowering," reviewed Ty.

"I want to order a couple of those vintage bottles to take back. Did you see those imperial stouts on the bottle list? I am picking up a couple of bottles of the Red Wine Barrel Aged Night Whale, and some Barrel Aged Penguins," Kareem stated, looking over the vintage beer list.

"It's been an exciting day, and I am eager to see what information these guys have tomorrow. Hopefully, we can figure out what was on their video and solve the mystery," said Ty.

"So far, it seems to be under the radar. Remember that with the Chupacabra, we had several witnesses. Champ had all the flyers around the town of the missing small animals and sightings on the news. Even the Red Ghost had some eyewitness accounts that made the local news, but so far, we only have the one video of this creature," presented Tegan.

"You're right. We may have to dig deeper online to identify others who may have seen this thing, or things. Remember, there were multiple individuals on that video. Who knows how many there are or what we're up against," said Carson.

"I will do some deep diving on the local news and internet searches," offered Kareem.

"Monitor the video's comment section too," suggested Ty. "Someone might post tips there."

CHAPTER 7

RIVERBOAT GAMBLER

The muffled sound of a car horn honking from the parking lot of the Batavia, Ohio Days Inn parking lot caused Ty to pull back the curtain and look outside. He saw Kareem and Tegan already in the car, the engine running, and waiting on him and Carson. He released the curtain and grabbed his wallet, ready to head down to them.

"Are you ready to go?" Ty yelled to Carson.

"Go on down. I'll meet you in the car. Almost ready," Carson responded from behind the bathroom door.

In the parking lot, the group awaited Carson's arrival for five more minutes while listening to Blessid Union of Souls, a band from Cincinnati, on the radio and planning their day.

The rear passenger door opened, and Carson got in beside Ty. Turning to give his friend the once-over, Ty commented on Carson's outfit.

"Where do you find these clothes?" he asked, shaking his head.

"What?" Carson returned, looking down at his hot-pink t-shirt reading *Chupacabra* with an image of the beast reminiscent of a Big Daddy Roth art style. "It's my newest subscription box called Cryptid Crate. It's a curated box featuring cryptozoology and paranormal merchandise. It's a shirt or maybe a hat, a book, a DVD, or some miscellaneous cryptid merch. It's my new favorite thing," responded Carson.

"Your new favorite? That's a hard list to crack. I know how you love your subscription boxes," Ty said teasingly.

"Sorry, guys. What's the plan?" asked Carson.

"Tegan found a coffee shop not too far away in Amelia. We are not meeting up with Buck and Parker for a few hours. That gives us time to explore the area, and it's always a great day when it begins with coffee," proclaimed Kareem.

Inside the small craft coffee shop of Crossroads Coffee at the intersection of Ohio Pike and Oak Street, the smell of premium small-batch coffee filled the air and brought a smile to the faces of the T.I.M.E. Agency. Each sitting in a large, oversized leather armchair around a rustic, red distressed painted reclaimed barn wood end table, Kareem got up to walk to the counter after the barista signaled their order was ready.

Tegan grabbed her Kirinyaga black coffee. Holding it close to her nose, she breathed deeply and enjoyed the aroma, then took a small sip and smiled, noting the intense, full-bodied flavor with almost-sweet overtones of tropical fruits, black currant, and berries. "They say this is one of the most complex and flavor-dense coffees in the world, and this cup doesn't disappoint," Tegan said. "One sip and I feel my body coming back to life," she said.

"There's something about a wonderful cup of coffee. Not the tired gas station brews that taste like sadness and disappointment, but a cup that brings joy from the first sip and ignites your taste buds. Coffee is a vehicle that connects all walks of life, regardless of your background," added Ty. His drink was a 50/50 blend of natural China Yunnan Fuyan and natural Colombia Anserma with notes of black cherry, raspberry, apple pie, and dark chocolate.

"Coffee is something I've been into longer than craft beer. Even when life wasn't working out as I expected and I felt often alone and depressed, coffee was a break from those moments. It always brought great conversations, memories, and hope," added Carson. "This chocolate raspberry has a nice body and a great flavor that allows you to kick back, relax, and forget your problems," replied Carson.

"Self-love is important," added Tegan.

"I prefer the single-origin coffee because it's often associated with higher quality and can be traced back to how and where it was grown," said Kareem. "I enjoy tasting the differences that climate and elevation can have on a coffee. A light or medium roast is what I drink. Sometimes the dark roast is nice, but it's too intense for my liking. The medium roast gives a delightful mix between sweet and intense, and the light roast can bring more vibrant, unique flavors out of coffees. It highlights the unique characteristics of a coffee's origin more than any other roasting styles. This one is a single-origin Ethiopian Yirgacheffe with crisp and vibrant floral notes and earthy undertones with hints of orange blossoms, lemon peel, honey, and black cherry finish," he added.

"Speaking of unique flavors," began Tegan, "Did you know that there is an annual cardboard boat race on the Ohio River in New Richmond?"

"Please tell me that's this week," responded Carson.

"No, but next best thing," she said. "There is a cardboard boat museum, and New Richmond is on our way to where we are meeting up with the guys from the Porkopolis Paranormal Society. It's a small museum inside an old car service station, but it's the world's only cardboard boat racing museum."

"Since we're here, I feel we have to check it out," replied Ty. "What d'ya say? Is it open?"

"It is open this morning and we don't need a lot of time. Maybe fifteen to twenty minutes, but that's what I was thinking. If it's the only one in the world and it's close to us, we have to see it," Tegan suggested.

As Tegan described, the museum was an old service station - with garage doors and concrete floors and brick walls. The museum's contents were hand-built boats used in the annual Cardboard Boat Regatta. People constructed these boats from everyday items like cardboard and duct tape, transformed into elaborate riverboats, dragon boats, and floating swan boats, then entered the race down the mighty, and sometimes mysterious, Ohio River.

It impressed Carson when the team entered the building. "When you said what this museum was about, and I heard cardboard boats, I envisioned cut-up cereal boxes or taped-up Amazon boxes. However, these boats are nothing like that. Built from large sheets of industrial-grade cardboard, these boats are seamless and well-constructed. Beautifully painted, wired with electricity, and depicting intricate steamboats, giant shoes, and sleek jets," Carson said as he looked at individual models.

"I also thought they would be small," said Ty. "Something like those remote-control vehicle races, but this is like a soapbox derby car. They are large enough to hold people as they float down the river," Ty added.

"There are some outstanding pieces here, but this one takes the cake," Kareem said as he moved closer to get a good luck at the replica of the Island Queen riverboat.

"Those large paddlewheel riverboats are an iconic symbol of the past on the Ohio River, and seeing a smaller version operating out there must be cool," replied Tegan. "But we should get going. It's about thirty minutes to Listermann Brewing to meet the guys."

Tegan pulled into the parking lot next to an industrial type building right off the Xavier University campus. Approaching the brewery, the group found a large area with picnic tables and large garage doors with televisions, a spacious room with a tap area, and an onsite restaurant. A large mural covered the outside wall of the brewery and depicted a colorful Super Mario Brothers scene, but spelled as *New Super Listermann Bros.* Carson's phone vibrated with a text from Buck stating he and

Parker were waiting inside the taproom. "Looks like they're already here," said Carson.

They decorated the inside taproom with a large wooden backdrop behind the taps. It had the type of intricate design Carson associated with antique French Victorian headboards. They continued walking into a room with eight large wooden picnic tables and another bright mural on the wall. It was a red, white, and black scene of people enjoying beer and conversation. A man at the end of the mural held a pint and the quote, *Bier ist gesund zu jeder*, meaning '*Whatever time of day it is, a glass of beer will do you good.*' The gang was ready for a beer and a conversation about what the Porkopolis team saw the other night. As they walked in, Buck shot up a hand.

"There are our guys over there," pointed Ty.

The two men stood up from the picnic table to greet their guests. Buck, a paunchy man with thick hands and a belly that overlapped the large buckle around his denim jeans, greeted the men with a vigorous handshake.

"Hey guys, thanks for meeting us today," he said. He looked at Tegan and tipped his Cincinnati Reds fitted baseball hat. "Ma'am."

Parker followed with a handshake of his own for each. He was a younger, taller man with a chinstrap beard and short brown hair under a backward facing snapback ball cap. His camo t-shirt with cut-off sleeves showed off his modestly muscular arms and thin frame. The group joined the paranormal investigators at one of the wooden tables.

Carson took a moment to take in the smell of the air inside the building. "Mmm… brewing day," he said with a smile after getting a whiff of one of his favorite smells in the world.

"We picked up some menus from the bar for you," replied Parker. Tegan glanced over the menu and knew she would order the Apricot Lemonade Parade Float, a wild kettle-sour fruited beer whose name reminded her of the cardboard riverboat regatta museum they visited.

"This brewery is pretty cool. It started out as a home brewery supply store back in 1991, but turned into a brewery in 2008. Their beer was in bottles before it ever saw a beer tap. When the homebrew shop first transitioned into a brewery, it was only through the sale of 22oz bombers in the store itself because you couldn't have a taproom yet back then. Over the years, the brewery has become a different place. They are now one of the more prolific centers of beer releases in Cincinnati with several new beers hitting shelves and fridges every single month. And I'll say the onsite restaurant makes a pretty mean Rueben," Buck said.

"I'm drawn to this Team Fiona New England IPA," said Kareem. "A combination of Citra and Centennial hops? I'm a huge hazy IPA fan, and the menu says it's for a good cause with proceeds supporting the Cincinnati Zoo and Fiona the Hippo. I see posts about her all the time on Facebook," he said.

"I like this session pale ale with Falconer's Flight hops sounds good. Plus, I like the name - Don't Talk Sh!t About Norwood," replied Carson. "That one will look good on the Untappd feed."

"A nice imperial stout always does the trick for me, although I see a smoked Bock on the menu too," replied Ty. "I'll start with the Cincinnatus stout," he selected. "What are you guys drinking?" he asked Buck and Parker.

"I'm a big IPA guy," replied Parker. "This Yoda Potato Strikes Back is one of my local favorites right now."

"If you fellers like IPAs, this place has a lot of them," said Buck. "I've been ordering this Amarillo, Citra and Vic Secret hopped I'm On a Boat. And being that they started out here by selling bottles, they have plenty of bottles and cans for sale if you want to take some back home," he added.

"We might have to have a second round because I see a Berliner Weisse on the board," Tegan replied.

"We might be here a while," said Carson. "Ty tells me ya'll have got some experiences. I'm interested in this video we saw from Chateau Laroche," Carson said to Parker. "Ty found the clip on YouTube and showed the rest of us."

"Anytime we have a video, the investigation is on fire," said Kareem.

"With the night vision, it was hard to see what we were looking at. You were the one who filmed it, right? What'd you see?" asked Tegan.

"That's right. We were on site to investigate ghosts. That's what we specialize in, and we've been trying to get inside the castle for a while. We got a call that we could come out, so we were all excited at the opportunity," Parker said. "Our two other members, Patti and Jocasta, were inside on the upper level. Buck was inside as well, but something drew me outside. I walked onto the patio, and I remember it was dark. I started feeling around to make sure I didn't knock something over because I knew if I did, we would never receive an invitation back to the property," he continued. "That's when I found a staircase leading down to the street. I crossed and walked through the grass that leads down to the river. Seemed like a good place to take a smoke break since I was down there and the investigation had been slow to that point. Then I heard a sound in the bushes that drew me closer in. I thought that was Old Man Andrews, the guy who built the place, so I wanted to get closer. As I turned the corner, I saw something. I didn't know what it was. It was hard to see in the moonlight, and I know how photos of unknown things always turn out, a little too far away and a little too blurry to make out what it is. That's when I decided I would get closer and started running toward the sound. I saw some objects, but I wasn't sure what I was seeing. I lost my concentration for a moment and that's when I tripped over a rock and went flying. My camcorder also went flying, but thankfully, it didn't break. Initially, the things I saw didn't notice me, but my sound startled whatever it was. Next thing I knew, there was a big, bright flash of light. I think that at least one of them had a thing in its hand that generated the flash. I don't know. It was so bright I closed my eyes and put my face in the grass for what I thought was a few seconds, but when I could see again, I saw it wasn't a few seconds, but more like twenty minutes," he said.

"That's when he came in and told us about the encounter. His battery died, so we had to give him another. We changed batteries, and he showed us the video when the camera came back on. We must have watched that footage a dozen times and couldn't figure out what he caught. It was not a ghost, but we couldn't debunk it because we didn't know what it was. We saw one creature raise what appeared to be a hand, then something it was holding emitted that bright light. When the light dissipated, the creatures were gone. We thought we saw three of them on the film and the girls thought they looked like giant frogs, but they were bipedal and looked about seventy-five pounds," added Buck.

"That's some shit," replied Ty. "I don't know what's scarier, a seventy-five-pound frog or one that is bipedal and holding a weapon."

"And how tall do you think this bipedal frog was?" asked Kareem.

"I'd say about three or four feet," said Parker.

"Roll that one around in your attic!" said Buck.

Carson looked at Buck nostalgically for a moment.

"My grandfather Patterson used to say that phrase. He used to hunt unknown creatures. He's who inspired me to research and investigate cryptids," Carson replied before taking a sip from his beer.

"Does he still help you with cryptids?" asked Buck

"No, unfortunately, he died not long after college. He went out into the woods to investigate a creature, but he didn't come back," stated Carson.

"Damn, sorry to hear that," replied Buck.

"Yeah, that was a hard one on me," Carson replied. "But I try to keep his memory alive by investigating these unknown creatures."

"This creature you captured on video, it doesn't have to roll around in my attic too much. That's a big ass frog," replied Ty.

"I don't want it anywhere around my attic. If there's one thing I hate, it's frogs," said Tegan. "They give me the willies! From the sound of your story, I would hate this one even more!"

"I've been racking my brain since I saw the video. I still don't know what it could be," said Kareem. "If we're thinking it's a frog, the largest frog in the world is a goliath frog, but it lives in a small habitat range in Cameroon and Equatorial Guinea. They are about thirteen inches from snout to vent and weigh up to seven pounds. Not nearly the size you described," considered Kareem.

"I know. Damnedest thing I've ever seen, and I've seen a lot of unusual paranormal shit that has no explanation explained," added Buck.

"I was a bit shaken up after it, and I've never felt that way hunting ghosts," admitted Parker.

"Ghosts are your specialty, and you are prepared for what they are and what you're expecting to see. If this is a cryptid, which I think it is because what we saw was a creature, that's unfamiliar territory for you, so you're unprepared and can't even process it," replied Carson. "Believe me, there are a lot of unknown things we still see and have trouble explaining. After we landed, we stopped at Bobby Mackey's for the ghost tour and there were things there we couldn't explain."

"That's a great place to investigate for ghosts. We always catch some good evidence there," replied Buck.

"We can say we've been there and done that now," added Tegan, "And I don't plan to go back. At least with cryptids, you can see them. Ghosts, it's an unseen enemy."

"Let me ask you this," began Ty. "You guys are from the area. How long have you lived here?"

"I was born here. My whole life has been in the Cincinnati area," replied Buck.

"Me too. Most of my life, anyway. We moved here when I was in elementary school," answered Parker.

"We came across a bunch of folders in one of our recent investigations," started Ty. "These folders were places that have had a high number of unusual creature sightings. What do you know about the Ohio Frogmen or the Loveland Frog?" asked Ty.

"That was one folder we found, and your sighting happened in Loveland, and you said these looked like frogs," added Carson. "Maybe there's a connection?"

"Nothing I've heard of," said Parker.

"I've heard it. Local legend around here. They have an annual run in town for the Loveland Frog. From what I remember, it was a couple of cops back in the seventies who seen something," answered Buck.

"The Loveland folder we found was rather small, but there were a few highlights, including the reports from the police officers. Prior to that, its first sighting occurred in the fifties. There have been occasional reports since the seventies, but maybe this is a reemergence?" theorized Carson.

"If it is the same creature, what happens in between?" wondered Tegan. "I mean, we have the mid-fifties and the early seventies. That's about twenty years aside from a random encounter. It's forty-five, almost fifty years since a solid, credible sighting," she commented.

"We don't know if those were legit sightings. Remember that cop walked back from his comments?" stated Kareem.

"Yes, but that has to be because of the scrutiny," Ty said. "You guys know that. People say they see ghosts or demons and friends and family think they're crazy," he said to Buck and Parker.

"Not only them, but now with the internet the skeptics have increased, and you know internet comments are often not friendly," replied Buck. "We get that a lot where someone calls us and before we can even get there to investigate, they call back and say don't come and assure us they saw nothing."

"Our benefit with this sighting is there is something on film. Even though it is a little blurry and once the camera falls, the grass partially obscures the frame," replied Tegan. "But it's a start, and that's more than we have with the sightings in that folder."

"You said those folders came from the investigation?" asked Parker. "Do you know where they came from? Like how they got to your site or who created them?"

"It was an underground government base," replied Carson.

"Yeah… I think it's time for the second round," added Tegan, still shaken from the memories of what she saw on that investigation.

"Secret government doings ain't anything new here," Buck stated.

"Like what?" asked Ty.

"For one, the Roswell crash. Area 51 got most of the publicity, but rumor is the government took those aliens to Wright Patterson Air Force Base up around Dayton. Less than two hours from us," replied Parker.

"And they used to have that TV show *Project Blue Book*, which was also from Dayton and focused on extraterrestrial investigations," added Buck.

"That's interesting and fits with what else we found on that investigation," said Kareem, looking at Tegan.

"I'm going up to get a drink. Anyone else want something?" asked Tegan. The guys placed their drink order with Tegan.

"From the brief notes in the files, this was something they dubbed in each of those sightings as the Loveland Frog. It disappointed me the folder didn't contain information that is more detailed. I had hoped it would give us further clues we could use in the field," replied Carson.

"Like I said, I've heard the name, but I never considered it an actual thing. There's the run, and they even had a musical a few years ago based on the Loveland Frog. But I figured those were urban legends and things to draw up tourism," said Buck.

"If the town is that into it, there must be something to the stories, right?" asked Kareem.

"Maybe. There's always some truth in rumors," replied Buck.

"Every legend has a beginning," said Carson.

Tegan returned with a Prehistoric Bowl Crusher Berliner Weisse, a Stylistic Abomination by Gummies Double New England IPA for Ty, Bananas in Paradise New England IPA for Kareem. Buck and Parker reordered the Yoda Potato and I'm on a Boat. Carson ordered the MannBeaverWolf Double Pastry IPA, thinking it sounded like a cryptid.

"I also bought a couple of six packs for us to have back at the hotel," Tegan said. "I thought we would enjoy this from the name, and based on the number of IPAs we've seen on the menu, I get it," she said as she sat down two packs of I've Had It With These Motherf*****g IPAs At This Motherf*****g Brewery. This one is a New England IPA.

"I don't think you can ever get enough of these MF'ing IPAs," replied Kareem.

"We need to find more eyewitnesses," said Ty. "You guys have been great, and it's important to get first-hand experience, but we still have little to go on. If you saw this thing… these things, perhaps someone else saw them," pondered Ty.

"No one was there at the castle. Not while we were there, at least," replied Parker.

"Anything on the news?" asked Kareem.

"Not that I've seen," added Buck.

Carson thought for a moment. "Let's search the internet when we get back to the hotel. Maybe send up a Google Alert to scan for anything recent on the Loveland Frog," suggested Carson. "Who knows what that might turn up, but that will prevent us from missing something."

"I recommend you go to the castle and see if there are any clues we may have missed," suggested Parker.

"Definitely on our list," Carson said as he removed a small notebook from his back pocket and jotted down notes.

Carson stood up and looked at the group. "I think I'm going to order a Rueben. Anyone?" asked Carson.

"Yeah, put me down for one too," said Ty.

The rest of the group jumped in on the same order. "I don't know if it's quintessential Cincinnati, but it's local, so I want to support it," said Carson.

"If you want to experience quintessential food in Cincinnati, do yourself a favor and go to Skyline Chili before you leave. I recommend the three-way," Buck said with a wink.

"Three-way? What kind of place is this?" asked Ty.

"They have three-ways, four-ways, and even a five-way," said Buck. "Many outside the area think it's a bizarre local specialty, but it is a staple of Cincinnati. The chili recipe has been unchanged since 1962. What makes it different from other chili is this one contains only meat, spices, and water. It doesn't come with onions, but you can add them. No beans either, but you can add kidney beans. It's the chili served on top of unseasoned spaghetti with a giant mountain of shredded cheddar cheese thrown on top. The chili gets a slight hint of sweetness from chocolate and cinnamon that helps cut through the savory nature of the cumin and chili powder, not to mention the vast amount of cheese that arrives on top. You can order a bowl of chili, but that's weird for most people. Many people also use the chili as a topping for a cheese Coney. You get the hot dog, bun, chili, and cheese. Top it off with mustard and onion and you're golden. That's not too different from other cities around the country, except maybe the enormous pile of cheese. What freaks visitors out is topping the spaghetti. That's the Cincinnati classic. There are three options for ordering Skyline in this fashion: a three-way, which is chili, cheese, and spaghetti, a four-way, which adds onions or beans, and then the five-way, which is both onions and beans. There is no wrong choice when ordering, but you have to make sure you have ample oyster crackers available when doing so," reported Buck.

"That's crazy. Is it a lunch or a dinner?" asked Tegan.

"Again, there's no wrong answer. Skyline is delicious at all hours of the day, but it's especially great after a long night out. You guys know, when you've had a beer, or five, do you care how aesthetically pleasing your hot dogs covered in cheese and chili are? No. You see the mountain of cheese, but as you get into the chili and the spaghetti, it's a magical combination that can't be beat," replied Parker.

"Be warned though, people will know if you're a first timer eating spaghetti in Cincinnati," replied Buck.

"How so?" asked Kareem.

"If you twirl the spaghetti on your fork, you are likely new to Cincinnati-style. Seasoned Cincinnatians cut the spaghetti with a fork, no twirling allowed," answered Buck.

"Sounds like we have to try it then," said Carson.

"I am as fascinated to try this spaghetti as I am to figure out what these creatures are. Both sound out of place," said Ty.

"There are a lot of strange things here in southern Ohio," replied Parker. "The river itself is a mysterious being."

"Yeah, a lot of things along or near the river. The Loveland Frog stories usually are near the water, but you also have the Crosswick Monster. That is another probable cryptid that's about twenty-five or thirty miles north of town. Then there was an incident in the Ohio River in the fifties or sixties where a woman who was swimming with a friend reported something unknown grabbed her in the river. When she came out, she had a large green outline of a handprint across her leg," reported Buck. "That was the Ohio River, but a little up yonder in Indiana."

"There are always stories of mysterious things in the river pulling people down. Some escape, some disappear," said Parker.

"If they find these things in or near water and are up to four feet and seventy-five pounds, I don't doubt they can pull someone under the water. From your story, Parker, you said it could hold something in its hands, so I bet it could use it to grab someone," speculated Carson.

Ty looked down at his cellphone after it vibrated. He clicked on an alert and scrolled through the information.

"Looks like we've got a hit," Ty said as he read the notification. "I created the Google Alert after your suggestion, Carson," he said. "I also set alerts for *Ohio Frog man* and *Cincinnati Frog*."

"And you picked up something?" Carson inquired.

"A couple of things. Some of these appear to be reposts of the older accounts we already know about. However, a few are recent. One from someone named Chandler Davenport and another from a woman named Vivian Gregory. Both are local bloggers that updated their site within the past week," said Ty.

"That sounds promising," replied Kareem.

"This blog from Vivian mentions something about a subway and says she encountered something while exploring the other night," read Ty.

"Subway? Here in Cincinnati?" asked Tegan.

"The country's largest abandoned subway is here," replied Buck. "It's underground and right downtown. Over two miles long. Few people know about it," he said.

"This story from Chandler says he spotted something at a place called Grand Valley Preserve," said Ty.

"The Little Miami River, which runs into the Ohio River, runs behind the preserve and also passes Loveland Castle," answered Parker.

"Let's try to reach out to both and see if we can arrange a meeting," suggested Carson.

"Both blogs have contact information for the author, so that it's doable," replied Ty. "I'll email them tonight and try to set something up."

"Guys, we have to get back to our team. We've got another investigation this weekend and need to get packed up and complete the arrangements," said Buck.

"We know how that is," replied Ty. "We appreciate you filling us in on the investigation at the castle and what you saw."

"And the tip on the Skyline chili," added Tegan.

CHAPTER 8

RACE STREET RENDEZVOUS

"**I**s this the place?" asked Ty as Carson brought the rental car to a slow crawl in front of a historic church, constructed in 1851.

"According to the GPS," Carson replied as everyone inside the vehicle wretched their necks to look at the well-preserved brick building now renovated into a three-story tap house. Ensuring no traffic was approaching, Carson paused for a moment in the street to take in the magnificent site of the old building before moving forward at a snail's pace and turning left onto West 15th Avenue where he found street parking next to a white wooden fence behind the building.

"We're about to find out," replied Kareem as they exited the vehicle and began walking to the corner of Race Street to meet their eyewitness.

"I guess this is it," responded Ty after noticing a text from Vivian Gregory. From the phone's disappearing preview, he could discern she was inside and awaiting the group's entrance.

Opening the door to the church-pub was even more impressive than its outside appearance. As the group climbed the tall steps leading to the main room of the bar, Tegan stared in amazement, and absorbed the architecture from inside the hallowed halls.

Reaching the top of the stairs, the dark-wooden balcony and banisters on the next level, ornate lighting fixtures, and wooden tables that appeared to be church pews sat in the back of the room near the historical alter, underneath the watchful eye of original nineteenth century art, caught everyone unaware.

As they entered the main floor, the large doors contained three custom circular glass windows. One read *Taft's* closed behind them. The name and origin story of the bar came from much of the local history and legend associated with President/Chief Justice William Howard Taft.

They stood at the edge of a large crowd of people, gathered to discuss their day amongst friends and enjoy some wonderful award-winning local beer, still drawn to the discovery of noticed artifacts and décor in every direction. Ty's concentration returned to his cellphone after the vibration signaled Vivian's response to his reply.

"She's in the back," Ty said as they walked deeper into the bar. "Over there," he said, pointing to a small cove of seating disappearing around the bend in the wall. Dark wooden floors, mahogany leather chairs, and a solid black distressed coffee table reflected the historic, yet dark and cozy vibe and offered a more secluded place to talk about unknown creatures. At least more so than the busy bar floor.

As the T.I.M.E. team knew too well, overheard conversations such as these could often lead to ridicule. However, Vivian described her encounter and published it to the public via her hobby-driven blog. The number of dedicated, hardcore, urban explorer fans who read her blog wasn't large, but its popularity had increased within its genre. And of that group, those interested in paranormal activity discussions would be a further minority.

Most, if not all, would find the unexpected experience of encountering unknown beings to be of interest, despite their lack of confidence in the paranormal, or at least in the unexplained world. One thing was certain, regardless of the number of readers, it was a sign that she would have no issue talking about her experience in front of others.

Walking to the back of the room, they found her alone at a small table and preventing the other customers from skootching the chairs away to their seat-deficient tables.

"Vivian?" Ty asked as they approached.

"Yes. Ty?" she asked in return.

"We're glad you had some time to meet up with us to discuss what you saw," he responded.

"I read your blog post. That was quite an amazing experience," added Carson.

"Yes, and unexpected," answered Vivian. "I've seen a lot of interesting things in my explorations, few animals. Maybe a stray cat, a raccoon, or something, but not anything like this."

"Where were you when you saw them?" asked Tegan.

"Close to here. At the abandoned subway system," replied Vivian.

"We only learned about the subway recently," said Kareem. "I did not know it existed."

"It's over a hundred years old, and sealed off, but it's a key to Old Cincinnati," answered Vivian. "It's exceptional to see if you have time. But if not, I can send Ty some information for another time," she added.

"We'll have to see how the week pans out," said Carson. "But that sounds like a must-see location."

"I don't know. I've had enough of forgotten underground facilities for a while, I think."

"Me too," answered Kareem.

"To get a feel for where you were, it's underground, dark, dusty, maybe the air is stuffy, and cooler than the aboveground atmosphere," said Carson. "That's different from what the guys with Porkopolis said about their encounter."

"Yeah, all of those things. In addition, I had already hiked through the entire complex and saw nothing. This was on the way back, close to the end of the line where I encountered them. It's as if they weren't there before. Maybe they came in behind me. I don't know. When I first arrived, I expected to run into someone. Usually you do, but when I didn't, I assumed it was all clear on the way back," Vivian replied. "But surprise!"

"I wasn't even there with you, and I am scared for you," said Tegan. "Of course, I am terrified of frogs, so if we relate it to these frogmen stories, I would totally freak."

"I don't know if they were frogs for certain, but they looked like frogs. No frog that I have ever seen, though. They were standing up and maybe four feet tall. If they weren't frogs, I mean they didn't have any hair, so I thought they were at least some kind of amphibian. When I saw them, I got an icy chill, which I don't get with frogs. Like I said, with urban exploring, you see some of those small critters."

"An icy chill?" repeated Ty.

"Yeah, like I didn't know what they were, but I could tell it wasn't a wonderful situation. I instantly thought fight or flight."

"Could you see what they were doing?" asked Carson.

"I don't know. They were in a room, then they were coming at me, so I got out as fast as I could," Vivian said.

"So they were aggressive to you?" asked Ty.

"I would have tried to ignore them, thinking my mind was conjuring things," she said. "But when they came after me, I knew they were not friendly, and I got out."

"You're lucky to have made it out of there," said Kareem.

"I know I'm not going back," Vivian replied, interrupted by an approaching person.

"You had a few minutes to look over the menu?" asked the young, anxious server, Jessika Mayer.

"I know my food choice first," he said, looking at his friends with a straight face, "For once!" he chuckled. "How about the Crispy Chicken Sandwich with tots?" he asked cheerfully. He looked at Ty and snarkily said, "I prepared ahead of time and read it online."

"I read it online too," said Ty, as he ordered a trio of tri tip sliders and loaded tots, then returned a smile at Carson.

Jessika pointed and motioned an extended finger between Carson and Kareem, "Oh hey, when you guys order your drinks, you get half off," acknowledging Carson's outfit consisting of a retro Austin Ice Bats t-shirt and a faded blue Cubs bucket hat with a band of Budweiser logos running across the middle, and Kareem's Beerburg Brewing shirt and jeans.

"Hey, no fair," said Tegan. "Why do they get fifty off?" she asked

"Because it's Taft's Tuesday, and anyone wearing brewery or beer apparel gets half-priced pints all day," Jessika added.

"Oh, damn. I wish I had worn my shirt from The Brewtorium," said Ty.

"Yea, I've got some shirts at home too," said Tegan. "And is that *really* beer apparel?" she asked as she pointed to the hat Carson was wearing. "It's more baseball than beer," she added.

"If it gets me a discount, it counts," Carson answered.

"If you need a shirt or some other merch, you can go over to Nellie's Tap Room and pick something up," Jessika added.

Kareem ordered a Cherrywood tri tip tacos combo, causing Tegan to feel the pressure of her turn arriving, resulting in a hurried selection of the fish 'n chips. It was an easy selection at any bar, Tegan thought, and unknown to her, the key indicator Carson used as a benchmark for every bar he ordered food from, regardless of its size. Even with little time to review the menu, she made a good choice.

"Have you looked over the drinks?" asked Jessica, ready to write their order.

Kareem ordered the Cherrywood amber, thinking it would bring out the flavor in the tacos. Carson, the Cold Boy pale lager, Ty chose the Gavel Banger IPA, Tegan picked Nellie's Lemon Frosty Ale, and Vivian concluded with the Hazy Cabana Juice IPA.

"Do you have the photos that you took in the subway?" asked Tegan.

"Yes, I brought the photos with me. I posted my story on the blog but haven't uploaded the digital images yet. I was going to upload them earlier today, but after you reached out to me, I figured I would hold on to them until you got to see them first," Vivian stated.

The images were dark and difficult to see, the explosion of light from the flash drenching the creatures in a white light that left them as a white outline on the image. What I saw from the first photo was two figures blanched in light. One appeared to be holding a tool that resembled a shovel. In the photo, one creature looked on as the other dug with the tool. She stated there were three in the room, but the closer individual blocked the third out of the image. The second photo showed the creatures after the flash. They turned their attention toward the unknown light source, and one was seen raising its arms in a menacing fashion.

"I remember the light caught their attention, but it also shocked them a bit. I don't think they are used to seeing light, and they were stunned. That gave me the gap I needed to escape," Vivian recalled.

The third image showed a shot taken behind her back as she began running toward the entrance of the subway. It showed the creatures regaining awareness and beginning to pursue her as she fled.

Each snap of the flash caused them to retract and increase the distance between her and the unknown beings, she reported. Subsequent images offered more lighting and detail of the pursuers. Even though the main room was still dark, there were places where light entered the larger area and gave the reviewers glimpses of the creatures' features.

"I'll be damned," said Carson as he picked up the photo and stared at it. "This one shows a closer look at one of them. It looks like a cross between a frog and the *Creature from the Black Lagoon*," described Carson.

"What's crazy is these earlier images show them standing. You can see their feet in this one," Ty said. "But these later ones where you are running back toward the entrance, they are on the ground like a frog."

"We pick up some more detail in this one where the flash appears to have misfired," Carson said, passing the photo to Kareem.

"It's hard to see because of the lack of flash, but you can see some of that natural light coming through and hitting the lead creature here. It's a little grainy, but it looks like one is wearing something around its waist. Like a bag of something," Kareem said, pulling the photo close to his face.

"So one is wearing something, one was digging something, and yesterday Parker said one was holding something that emitted light," described Tegan.

"Frogs that are not only bipedal but have opposable thumbs allowing them to hold and use tools," compiled Carson. "That's why cryptozoology is so fascinating to me. These things are creatures that you saw and chased you, so you know they are real things, yet the descriptions of their actions reveal traits and characteristics traditional science says is impossible."

"I've run up on animals in the woods, and even animals that are dangerous or have the potential to harm. I was cautious, but not scared. These things I didn't know what they were, but I was terrified," Vivian replied.

"And the fact they gave chase shows your instincts were correct," said Tegan.

"The old accounts that were classified as or attributed to the Loveland Frog are of a creature scared and running away. But after we saw the video, I searched online and found on at least one occasion, the witness claimed something struck them," remembered Carson.

"And we know they are agile. The documented sightings wrote these frogmen could leap over the guardrail," added Ty.

"Multiple reports also mentioned the light-producing wand, so the ability to hold an object is consistent," said Carson.

"I remember reading one eyewitness report saying he saw three frog men that looked like trolls with tight-fitting clothes," said Tegan. "Maybe these tight-fitting clothes resemble what looks like a bag on its waist in the photo?" she suggested.

"Could be," responded Carson. "These sightings have been at night and from a distance. We must consider what people reported seeing isn't completely accurate. That adrenaline rush that happens when you first see something you weren't expecting and can't identify causes the mind to embellish details and allows an overactive imagination to take it from there."

"When you entered the subway, did you close the door behind you?" asked Kareem.

"No, pretty sure I left it open. It's usually padlocked, but when I got there, it was unlocked," Vivian recalled.

"So these frogmen could have been in there already, or maybe entered after you?" followed Kareem.

"I didn't see them when I entered, but I guess they could have already been there. I had to pull the door open, but maybe they found another way in, or could enter the open door after I was inside. I was in there several hours, so it's possible," Vivian responded.

"I'm thinking about their actions," Ty said as he went over scenarios in his mind. "In the old police reports, they had an object we are calling a wand that emitted and allowed them to run away. In Parker's video, we saw the light, but then they were gone. Like they use that light to create a distraction or temporarily blind someone so they can make their escape. You didn't mention a wand and instead of escaping, they came after you," Ty added.

"Or we could say they were trying to escape. They were in an enclosed room and Vivian was in the doorway. Their only escape route would be through her," Carson said.

"Yes, but once in the main room, they continued after her. Why not run in the opposite direction? They may not have had an exit, but they would be away from the perceived threat from the human?" followed Ty.

"You said we only know of one prior witness who claimed the creature attacked," said Ty. "What was that about?"

"That was the women in Evansville, swimming in the Ohio River, but we can't be certain that's related to the Loveland Frog," claimed Carson. "Remember those notes we saw about the Shawnahooc? The demon that the Twightwee believed guarded the riverbanks of the Little Miami and chased away anyone who came into its territory? Now that may have been stories to keep the French out of the Twightwee land, but the description is similar to what we've seen with the frogmen."

"It would be cool if we could check out the room in the subway system," suggested Ty. "As well as Loveland Castle. I would like to look around the area where the police spotted the creature in the fifties and seventies, even though we have had no recent sightings there. Might still give us a look at the area and maybe some context."

The number of sites the group needed to investigate was growing, even with Chandler yet to meet, causing Carson to speculate that they would need to split into two groups to cover the ground.

"Looks like we've got our work cut out for us," said Carson. "We'll have to work out the logistics and plan to investigate the sighting locations."

"We need to identify what these creatures are, why they are here, and how dangerous they might be. Hard, physical evidence is the only way to answer those questions," commented Ty.

"You've got my number," said Vivian. "Please reach out if you need anything else," said Vivian. "I also have this," she said, handing Ty a piece of paper with a sketch layout of the Cincinnati subway and details on how to get to the entrance. "If you explore it."

"Much appreciated," Ty said.

Looking at her watch, Vivian stood up and was ready to leave. "I've got to meet up with someone I'm interviewing for my blog update. We are talking about exciting urban exploring locations around town," Vivian said.

"I'm not sure your guest will top your recent experiences," replied Kareem.

"Maybe not, but I am always looking for unknown places. I will not let some overgrown seventy-pound frog keep me away," she said.

At the corner of Turrill Street and Blue Rock Street, Carson pulled in front of another church. This time, it was the historic St. Patrick church building. The Gothic Revival church, built in the 1890s, wasn't as old as the church housing Taft's Ale House, but its flying buttresses and brick facades covered with sculptured concrete resembling sandstone, reflected a common look of churches from that era, and Cincinnati had plenty of them.

"Another historic church resurrected into a brewery?" asked Ty.

"Ben Franklin said *'Beer is proof that God loves us and wants us to be happy,'*" added Carson.

"That's paraphrased," mentioned Ty. "Wasn't exactly what he meant."

"It's printed on t-shirts and plastered across the internet. Good enough for me," argued Carson. "I love scoring this free street parking. We are fortunate today!"

"What's the story with this place?" asked Kareem.

"This is called Urban Artifact, and the brewers wanted to focus on the relationship between art, music, and beer," said Carson.

"Sounds like a great time to me," replied Kareem.

"The building is in a centralized neighborhood. There's a big local art community already present, and music was part of this neighborhood's DNA. I read they could convert the former school's gymnasium into a brewhouse and the parish's basement into a taproom. When I read about this place, I thought this would be perfect for Tegan. They specialize in historic tart and sour ales," Carson added.

"That sounds amazing," responded Tegan. "Can't wait to check it out!"

Inside, they found the taproom and listening lounge, where flyers on the wall advertised live music every Wednesday through Saturday nights and had a capacity for two hundred patrons. Outside, between the church and rectory, a beer garden provided room for more customers. Looking around as they entered, they saw the former sanctuary upstairs on the main floor of the church provided an event space for concerts, theater, and other events.

"I'm impressed. Many people don't like sours and tart beers the way I do," stated Tegan. "And this many on the menu is incredible."

"I read that the brewery is focused on educating customers on these styles, and in the tap room they list the pH level of each beer instead of IBU. For those who think it is too tart, they offer hop syrup and raspberry syrup to help level out the acidity," replied Carson. "They also aim to bring back a lot of old beer styles that died with Prohibition."

"Prohibition, jazz, and a lot of reclaimed materials like these old radiators, marble slabs, pipe and elm tables, and the 1930s-era lamps give it a step-back-in-time vibe," said Ty. "Adding arts, culture, and celebratory events here collaborates with that vibe."

Stopping by the taproom, the group reviewed the menu behind the bar. With so many options of her favorite beer style, Tegan found herself in heaven. In most craft breweries, it often limited her to one or two varieties if she was lucky. This was a first for her, a menu only devoted to sours. She selected the Spyglass - a lemon-lime sour fruited Berliner Weisse. Kareem selected the Paperweight, made with three-thousand pounds of apricots. Ty went with an offering that he hadn't seen before, a Grape Ale with Astrolabe with three-thousand pounds of Concord grapes and fifteen grams of vanilla beans. Carson wrapped up the order with a Gas Light double IPA with a tart background, using ingredients from the Ohio Valley.

"Pinch me, I must be dreaming," said Tegan. "I would love to try every one of these beers. Rarely do I get a wide selection of sours," she said as she led the way outside to the beer garden and located a table.

Taking a seat at a picnic table beneath an enormous umbrella in a grass-covered yard surrounded by huge shade-giving trees, the group surmised it to be one of the best places in the city to sit outside with a beer.

"We still have several places to check out during this investigation, but it has to be right near the top of the list," rationalized Kareem.

"Now that we've met with two witnesses, maybe we can start plotting our next steps," said Tegan.

"We know most of the sightings have occurred around water. The Little Miami River runs next to Loveland Castle, and Parker said he saw them close to the river. Those old accounts from the police officers and the businessperson who first spotted the creatures were in wooded areas close to the river, and that other witness you found, Chandler Davenport, reported seeing them around water as well," added Kareem.

"Right, and I looked on the map to the place where the subway system Vivian told us about was located, and it's not next to water, but close to it. You have the Ohio River a few miles away, but also Mill Creek that runs a short distance from the entrance," replied Carson.

"Speaking of Chandler," said Ty, "We're all set up to meet with him tomorrow and talk about his experience at the reservoir. He's going to meet us at MadTree Brewery, which is about ten miles from the location he saw them, but he works part time at the brewery and said we could meet up with him during his lunch break," reported Ty.

"Beer and cryptids sound like a brilliant combination to me," replied Carson. "I can't wait to learn more about these creatures tomorrow!"

CHAPTER 9

CINCINNATUH WARSHROOM

At a wooden table in the sunlight alcove behind the blue door of 6930 Miami Avenue's Coffee Please, Carson flipped through the pages of the *Cincinnati Enquirer* searching for any updates on the mysterious frogmen and awaiting notification that his white chocolate salted caramel latte was ready. In the middle of the shop, the roasters generated amazing smells that caused Kareem to close his eyes and deeply inhale the moment.

"Love it! I simply love it," Kareem said. "Such a quaint little shop. I love the feel of the interior space. Rustic and homey." He opened his eyes to take a bite of the magical delight called the Puffin Muffin - a large muffin with cinnamon and nutmeg covered in sugar. "I know we will eat soon, but you know me. If I don't have something for breakfast, I get hannngry," he added with an elongated pronunciation.

"That you do, my friend. That you do," replied Tegan as she rejoined the table after walking around to check out the store's offerings. "I love the menu as well. It's why I love smaller shops. Everything is more boutiquey and personable."

"Speaking of food," Ty said as he brought everyone's drinks to the table, "We're supposed to meet Chandler at MadTree later today. He is the opening bartender at eleven and I noticed down the street is a Skyline Chili. After what Buck and Parker told us the other day, a three way before meeting Chandler sounds like a necessity."

Ty distributed a Tanzania Peaberry to Kareem, a Colombia-Papua New Guinea-Nicaragua blended local favorite called Madeira's Choice to Tegan, Carson's latte, and kept a mug of the smoky, caramelly Bali Blue French Roast for himself.

"Cream?" Ty asked, placing a green and blue glazed ceramic creamer in the center of the table next to a wicker basket of sweetener options.

"Heading to Skyline for an early lunch works out great," responded Carson. "Keep's the hunger monster that is Kareem away and gives Chandler a chance to settle in before we interrupt."

"Anything in the paper about those creatures?" asked Tegan.

"Nothing so far. I hope the Google Alerts keep us abreast of any recent developments. However, we need to keep our eyes and ears open for clues. You never know where or when something might drop in our lap," replied Carson. "And I am hoping we can put boots on the ground tomorrow in terms of an investigation."

"Now that I have had my morning coffee and a muffin, I'm ready to start the day," replied Kareem. "Bring on the weird mystery frogs."

"My grandfather used to say, *be careful what you wish for*," answered Carson.

"We've learned that even when you have a plan, prepare for the unexpected," stated Ty.

"I'd rather not find them," Tegan said. "Bipedal frog men sound even more creepy than regular frogs."

The sand-colored building with yellow, blue, and red accents, fronted by a large-faced clock, looked small from the front, but the depth of the building displayed its size. A large dining room contained tables, chairs, and booths to accommodate the large number of patrons that frequented the franchise. There was also the option to sit at the counter near employees preparing the food. As the group looked around to take in the ambience, a server appeared at the table.

"Good morning. Can I get y'all started on some drinks?" asked a petite blonde-haired woman with her hair in a ponytail.

"Sweet tea," started Carson.

The order soon repeated around the table.

"Comin' right up. I'll give a few minutes with the menu," the server said, turning toward the centrally located service island. Carson watched as workers behind the island assembled orders already taken, working to prepare the regional legend. As quickly as the server left, she returned with a tray carrying four large plastic cups filled to the rim with sweet tea.

"First time here?" she asked with a hopeful smile.

"Yes, but I think we're ready. We all want to try this three-way we've heard so much about," spoke Ty.

"Good choice. One of our signature dishes," she said. She didn't need to write the simple order down, returning once again to the kitchen. The group turned to watch her and the staff prepare the order, while also noticing the counter near the front of the dining room where customers took the meal ticket and paid another staff member. The food prep took only a few minutes before it was on a tray and headed back to the group's table.

"Wow!" said Kareem as the server placed the tray in the center of the table.

The three-way arrived almost immediately, each in an oval platter that contained a mound of spaghetti, warm chili that filled the bottom of the serving dish infusing the pasta in a delicious soup, and topped with a heaping portion of cool cheddar, creating the perfect marriage of hot and cold with each bite. A medium-sized bowl of oyster crackers offered the perfect additive to soak up the juice from the chili.

"We should get a selfie of our first three-way before we eat it," suggested Kareem.

He positioned his cell phone to capture everyone seated in the booth with the plate of spaghetti and the kitchen behind them.

"This looks fantastic!" Tegan said, as she was the first to dive her fork into the depths of the cheese mountain.

"Remember, the guys from Porkopolis said not to twirl the spaghetti on your fork, else we'll look like a tourist," said Kareem.

"That's right," replied Tegan, adjusting her approach to cutting the spaghetti with the fork's edge. "It's unnatural to me, but we want to blend in," she added.

Kareem, a self-declared foodie, took a bite with the look of a librarian searching the vast annals of a collection to retrieve the perfect book. "I can't quite place it," he said. "No onions or beans in this one, and I get water, meat, and spices, but it has a unique blend of seasonings. It's sweet. Maybe some cumin? Paprika? Maybe a bit of vinegar and some cloves. Maybe cinnamon?" he trailed off in his exploration of ingredients.

"That's a family secret," said the server, returning to place the bill on the table. "The founders' lips are sealed on that one. I don't even know what's in it," she said. "No hurry on the bill, but pay up front when you're ready," she said, pointing to the cashier island.

"It's like a soup or meat stew," replied Ty as he opened two bags of oyster crackers and crumbled them on top of the platter before stirring them into the spaghetti. "But it's delicious," he replied as the crackers soaked up the liquid.

"Excellent portions," added Carson. "I can see why this is so popular. Especially late at night after a few drinks. This would do the trick."

"We're open until 2 a.m. on Friday and Saturday," the server said before leaving to make the rounds and checking in on the other tables.

"It's a good, quick meal, too. And that's good because we should get going if we want to get to MadTree before it gets too busy," suggested Tegan as she looked at the time on her phone.

"I'll take care of this," Ty said as he stood up and picked up the check.

The server walked over to say goodbye to the guests. "If you're in town for a bit, you should go for the Trifecta," she said.

"What's the trifecta?" asked Kareem.

"Skyline, Graeter's Ice Cream, and LaRosa's Pizzeria. All Cincinnati legends.

"I love pizza and ice cream," replied Kareem. "We'll keep that in mind!"

"It's only half a mile to the brewery," said Carson. "Seems almost crazy to drive."

"True, but what are we doing after MadTree?" asked Ty, rejoining the team.

Traffic buzzed and hurried past the group as they walked the half mile to MadTree Brewing, although they still focused on the spaghetti.

"That spaghetti hit the spot. I can see why it's so popular here," said Tegan. "While we are in Ohio, we should hit up White Castle too."

A wince flew across Carson's face, pausing for a second, and then disappearing. Ty, Kareem, and Tegan continued to discuss the meal and future options, but Carson walked in silence.

Fifteen minutes after beginning their journey along Madison Road, they arrived at their destination, walking through the outdoor patio with a large brick wall with an open window spacing on one side and a metal beam that made it look like construction had stopped in progress at one time. As they walked inside the brewery and headed toward the bar, Carson scanned the interior of the building, as if he were searching for the nearest exit.

This soon after opening, the crowd had not yet arrived. The bar was empty, with only a lone thin, salt-and- peppered haired-patron sitting near the end of the bar, and a young man with a hat and sunglasses at a nearby table eating an order of Nati Twist. The team took a spot in the center of the bar as Chandler Davenport had his back turned, busily wiping down empty pilsner glasses from the dishwasher. Hearing the seats move, he placed the glasses on the rack for their next opportunity for action.

"'Morning! What can I getcha?" he asked with an eager greeting.

"Chandler? I'm Ty. We messaged each other on Facebook."

"Yes, Ty. How are you? Glad you guys could make it," Chandler said, looking at each member of the group and nodding as he shook Ty's hand.

"Must be pretty lonely here first thing in the morning," said Carson.

"Yes, it's slow at opening. A bit of a bump during lunch, but most of the crowd shows up in the afternoon. We've got a pretty good happy hour menu if you stick around," Chandler replied. "Otherwise it's me and old Mango here today."

"Mango?" asked Kareem.

"His name is Cary, but we all call him Mango," replied Chandler with a wide smile, pointing toward the end of the bar. The man a few seats away nodded to the group. "Mango."

"On account of me always eating mangos," interrupted the man.

"I love mangos too," said Kareem.

"Probably not the same mangos," replied Chandler. "Up here we call green bell peppers *mangos*," he added.

"But why are they called…" Kareem asked.

Chandler shrugged, "Dunno. One of those Ohio things. Anything you see on the menu before we get into it?"

"PsycHOPathy for me," answered Kareem, turning towards Tegan with a smirk. "The name entices me."

"I bet it does. Which reminds me, when are you going to come see me for a counseling session?" asked Tegan. "I know we have things to discuss."

"I don't know. I thought that since we are close friends and work together, maybe it wouldn't be a good idea. I've got a lot of things in my head now and I don't know if I'm ready to deal with it or if you would be too close to the situation to be unbiased," answered Kareem.

"Unbiased? You always have known me to be not only open and loyal but also honest. It doesn't help to sugarcoat things. I'll give you honest feedback, even if telling you what to hear isn't what you wanted to hear. And you know you can tell me anything," Tegan said.

"Well," said Ty, clapping his hands together once. "That took a weird turn from ordering a drink," he observed. "I'll have the Thundersnow."

"That's an excellent Scottish Ale," replied Chandler. "One of the best around the state, I'd venture to say."

"I'll have that double IPA," Carson said, pointing to the menu.

"Phantom Forest, comin' up," said Chandler. "And for the lady? My bad, I should have taken you first."

"It's okay," Tegan said. "I know better than to get between Kareem and an IPA. Typically, I'd go for the sour, but I had a lot of them already. I need a little balance. I'll get the Odin's Breath IPA."

"You said you saw something the other day at the Preserve," began Ty.

"Yes, that's a nice place out there. Camp Dennison Nature Trail runs through there where you can hike, fish, kayak, and catch some cool wildlife," answered Chandler. "It's close to where I live, but being there feels like you are out of the city, even though it's only ten minutes outside Cincinnati."

"Does it get many people out there?" asked Tegan.

"Sometimes, yes. It's a popular spot. That night there weren't too many. I think the Reds were in town. Plus, it's gated, and you must have Indian Hill water service to get access," Chandler recalled. "I was taking in the trails to decompress after a busy week here."

"Sounds like a good place to accomplish that," said Kareem.

"A few minutes there does the trick, but not that night," Chandler said.

"What was different about this night?" asked Carson

"It was a little quieter than normal, and it wasn't a lack of people," said Chandler. "It was the whole place. No bugs chirping, no birds, and no wildlife. I didn't even see a squirrel. It wasn't dark, yet but getting late in the afternoon on an overcast day. The tree-covered areas were darker, but it wasn't difficult to see."

"And what did you see?" asked Carson, the wince flashing across his face once again.

"Three figures," said Chandler. "Looking back later, I called them humanoids because I didn't know what else to call them."

"What did these humanoids look like?" Ty asked

"They were standing on two legs, which is why I stared at them. I could tell them were not human, and I don't know many animals that stand comfortable on two legs. Not for a long period at least," Chandler said. "And these guys were comfortable walking around. It was like they were looking for something."

"What do you think they were looking for out there?" followed Tegan.

"I don't know. As I got a little closer, I stopped. I thought they were frogs, but that made little sense because they were standing up and were larger than any frogs I have ever seen," Chandler stated.

Tegan shivered at the thought of ordinary frogs ran through her mind. However, these were no ordinary frogs, and she knew their paths would meet.

"Did you get any photos, or maybe a video on the cell phone?" asked Carson.

"No. I didn't bring my phone with me. The battery was dead, so I left it in the car and headed up the trail," Chandler replied. "But I got a good look at them. And likely, I will never forget it."

"When you saw them searching for something, did they find anything? How were they searching for it?" asked Kareem.

"One looked like it had a tool, like maybe a shovel, to dig at the ground," Chandler recalled. "And one had like a stick in his hand. Honestly, I thought it was a wand," he said.

Ty and Kareem looked at each other and recalled Vivian had a similar description of the creatures in the tunnels beneath the city.

"Definitely some similarities to other accounts we've heard," Ty said.

"This wand-like object, did it do anything?" asked Kareem.

Chandler shook his head. "I don't know. When I saw its hand go up, I turned and made a brisk break for the car," he said before turning to attend to a new customer who ventured up to the bar.

Carson stood up and rubbed his stomach as an uncomfortable look graced his face.

"You okay?" asked Ty.

"Yeah, but that chili is talking to me," Carson replied as he looked around and dropped his credit card on the table. "If Chandler brings the bill, settle up for us. I'm gonna hit up the bathroom."

"Where is the preserve in relation to the Loveland Castle?" Tegan asked.

"Loveland? It's up the pike a bit," answered Chandler. "Not too far. Less than ten miles."

"What would bring these creatures out to the preserve?" Kareem wondered aloud.

"We know they like water, right, if we go on the assumption that they are frogs," said Tegan.

"We don't know they are frogs," replied Ty. "They look like frogs, but frogs aren't four feet tall."

"Thank God," said Tegan, again shivering at the thought of them.

"Bipedal and able to use tools? They are advanced," said Kareem.

"And digging. That's two accounts that mention digging. Digging means they are searching for something. Something buried, but what?" asked Ty.

"Searching means they have cognitive abilities, and the ability to use a tool suggested they are an advanced species," stated Carson.

"Has anything changed in the area?" asked Kareem.

"In town? Things have grown up around here. Lots of construction. The change is vast," Chandler replied.

"What about the preserve itself?" returned Kareem.

"The other night we had a pretty reasonable storm. That might have stirred up activity in the area. I can't recall anything since they reconstructed the preserve. That storm was a harder one than we've had in some time," Chandler stated.

"What reconstruction?" asked Tegan.

"It's a former gravel excavation site," said Chandler. "They combined the previous separate lakes to form one large lake. A great location for canoeing and fishing."

The man at the end of the bar stood up and dropped twenty dollars on the counter, then walked behind the group.

"Lemme sneak by ya'," said the man, now noticeable tall.

Ty and Kareem drew their seats in, closer to the bar.

"You're fine," the man said as he made it past them.

"See ya next time, Mango," Chandler called out to the man. "Glad to see the Bengals games are back on. We'll have the game on and some goetta for breakfast."

"Who Dey!" the man exclaimed as he disappeared around the corner.

In the men's room, the bathroom door opened.

"*Ocupado!*" Carson called out from the stall.

The sound of running water in the sink soon drew Carson's attention. The next sound was that of the handle reaching the bottom of its range of motion, followed by a series of brief gurgling noises, and the sudden rush of 1.6 gallons of water. The door creaked as Carson emerged, nodded to the occupant of sink number one as he made his way to the second sink. Carson turned on the water, wetted his hands before plunging the hand soap twice times and returned his hands to the warm water as he lathered his hands in a slow, circular motion.

"Hey," he softly stated uncomfortably.

"Hey," returned the tall man from the sink number one. "Sorry to catch ya' coming out of the commode like this," he said. "But those creatures you were talking to Chandler about, I saw them too. A few nights ago," the man side.

"You did?" Carson recognized his sink-mate as the man from the bar. "It's... Cary, isn't it?" Carson asked as he dried his hands on a paper towel.

"That's right. Or Mango. I answer to either."

"Okay... Mango. I'm Carson," he said. "So were you at the preserve too?" asked Carson.

"No, I was out on Adams Road up in Loveland. It's about eight miles off from Camp Dennison. Little Miami Scenic Trail runs through the woods and it's shady, plus damp, in certain areas. I spend a lot of time in the woods walking around and hunting morels."

"Morels? Like mushrooms?" asked Carson.

"Yeah, they're plentiful around these parts," Mango replied. "I can spend the better part of a day searching for them. I have my old newspaper boy back with a sack of mangos and a few bottles of water. Maybe I will sneak in a bottle of pop or two. That's why they started calling me Mango. I cut the morels and put them in a brown paper bag instead of a paperboy bag. That bag has proven to be one of the most useful things I've ever had. Easy to sling over your shoulder and carry the whole day's bounty," he said.

"Bounty? Do you get a lot of mushrooms?" asked Carson.

"Lately, yes. That storm helped bring 'em out. That's where I was when I seen them creatures. I was in a heavily wooded area. Then I looked up and saw something I had never seen in all my years in the woods. Three, what looked like standing frogs, walking around off to the side on one of the grassy banks," Mango stated.

"One of our earlier eyewitnesses said they encountered them near Loveland Castle," said Carson.

"I wasn't too far from there. This time I was on the walking trails around Ertel Run. It empties into the Little Miami River and from there it's close to the Castle if you take the Scenic Trail. I was following the river, ended up out near Adam's Road. Out there in the boonies, where I can get my fill of morels. Few people know my secret spots, and I like to keep it that way," said Mango.

"What do you remember about that night?" asked Carson.

"It was warm out. I planned to go out that morning before noon, but I got behind with other things and got a later start that I liked. I knew I had been out there a while, so there would be a lot of shrooms. I like to go early in case someone accidentally finds my area. My feet were getting a little tired because I was working on breaking in a new pair of tennis shoes, so I was already walking slow. However, the humidity was something. I ended up taking off my shirt and tucking in through a loop in my britches," replied Mango.

"That humid this time of year?" clarified Carson.

"Yeah, after that storm it was muggy and I get warm easily," responded Mango.

"You said you were out there several hours. It was humid, and you were tired," repeated Carson. "Do you think maybe you were too tired and were seeing things?"

"I'll tell ya what. I've been in these same woods for a long time. I've seen a lot of things. A lot of unusual things at that," Mango said. "But I ain't seen nothing like those things. Blew my mind."

"You said they looked like frogs. You got a good look at them?

"Yep, sure did. They looked a little like a frog from what I first seen, but I knew that tweren't right on account of they were on two legs. There were three of them and they looked 'ta each have something different," replied Mango.

"Like what?" asked Carson.

"One had a stick like thing, another a little shovel, and the other had a bag around him, kinda like I had. I don't think he was putting mushrooms in the bag as I was, but they were looking for something. One thing that was odd about them is they had one arm looked slimmer than the other," recalled Mango.

"From the people we've talked to, we think that whatever they are, they are looking for something. Reports are only every few decades, so maybe they disappear for a while, then return to search for... whatever it is they are looking for," theorized Carson.

"Might could be! Maybe they hibernate like them cicadas and come back every seventeen years," suggested Mango.

Carson didn't reply, but shook his head in agreement.

"Well, buddy. I won't keep ya! I gotta swing by the carry out and do some Krogering on the way home. But I saw you head this away, and I wanted to catch ya before you guys left. Let you know what I saw," Mango concluded.

"I appreciate the info. Every little bit helps, and I think we're going to head out tomorrow to check out some of these areas," Carson replied.

"What's taking Carson so long? Maybe he fell in. Should someone go check on him?" asked Tegan.

The bathroom door opened, and Carson began walking back to the bar.

"I had the most interesting bathroom conversation in my life," replied Carson.

"Interesting? In the bathroom? How so?" said Ty.

"Let's get out of here. There's another place I want to hit up while we're on this side of town. I'll tell you on the way," Carson answered.

The drive was a short one, about six minutes to Nine Giant Brewing, but enough time to fill the team in on the details Mango Cary provided.

"We have another point on the map where there is a verified sighting," Carson said as they walked toward the brick-faced building.

"Now we have to connect the points and look for our investigation area," replied Ty.

"I think we have enough to start with an initial investigation. I'd like to start with Camp Dennison and see where we are after that. Chandler's encounter there was recent, and it puts us a little further down river," said Carson.

"True. The subway seems to be the outlier because it's further away from the others, although it's also close to the river," said Ty.

"I think Camp Dennison is a good place to start. It intrigued me that Chandler saw the creatures using tools and digging in the area," replied Tegan.

"Vivian saw them doing that also, but it was underground. Chandler said the lake at Camp Dennison was once multiple separated lakes, but they converted them into one. I think these creatures are looking for something. They returned to the area, but it's changed, so they had to dig for what they were looking for," added Kareem.

A woman approached them at the bar. Young, blonde, and with a slight country drawl, Cora Morrison poured a glass of water for each of the newly seated guests.

"Speaking for looking for something, what I can get 'cha, sugar?" she asked Kareem.

Scanning the menu, he spoke without looking up. "We're here for a few beers," he replied, then looked up at the bartender.

"That's great - how 'bout an IPA?" asked Cora.

Kareem smiled at the suggestion. "It's like you read my mind," he replied.

"The Interstellar Drift is one of my favorites right now," she recommended.

"Sold," replied Kareem.

She moved down to Ty. "How about you, handsome? How are you?"

"Fine, how are you?" Ty returned.

"I'm dandelion," she said with a flirtatious smile.

Ty scanned the menu choices before settling on a lovely porter. "West End Girls," he ordered. Tegan began humming the tune of the popular eighties pop song by the same name.

"How about you, honey-bunny?" Cora asked to the still-humming Tegan.

"I sat myself back to true north with the IPA last time. Back to my Berliner Weisse. I can't pass up Save Ferris," Tegan said. "One of my favorite movies of all time."

"And what about you, cowboy?" Cora concluded.

"Well, I don't know about cowboy, but I am thinking a smooth blonde sounds good right now," Ty replied.

"I can make that dream a reality for you!" she said with a wink before continuing, "You coulda been a cowboy. Ropin' and ridin'. Singing campfire songs…" she said.

"I'm not much of a singer, but I enjoy a campfire and telling stores," Ty stated.

"Ghost stories? Monsters in the night?" she asked.

"That's not far off," replied Ty.

She distributed the drinks to her patrons, ending with the blonde ale, I Like Beeer!

"Matter of fact, we're up here from Texas checking out one such campfire story," Ty added before leaning in closer. "You haven't seen anything strange and unusual around here, have you?" he asked in a hushed voice.

"Strange and unusual? You'll have to be more specific around here," she said with a chuckle. "I've seen a lot that fit that description."

"He's talking about frogs. Giant four-foot bipedal frogs that hang around the Little Miami," stated Kareem.

"Sounds like the Loveland Frog," Cora answered.

"You know about them?" asked Tegan.

"Sure, I've heard of 'em. Every one's heard of them. They have a triathlon here each year, the festival, and they made a musical about it a few years back. Nothin' to it, though. Only rumors and a way to pique the public interest," she dismissed.

"I'm not so sure," answered Carson. "Seems like there has been a sudden increase in sightings around town, and that's what we're here to investigate."

"Oh, you guys are investigators? Like those guys on the television? What do they call that? Crypti-crypto…"

"Cryptozoologist," stated Carson.

"I thought that was make believe. I never met a crypto-zoo-ologist or whatever," Cora said.

"There are a lot of unknown things out there," replied Kareem. "Especially after dark."

"The freaks come out at night?" teased Cora.

"Sometimes they do," answered Tegan. "Sometimes they do." She took a long drink of the tart Berliner Weisse as she pondered the possibility of the days to come. She starred at the glass after sitting it back on the bar counter, holding her gaze for what seemed like several minutes. "How bad could it be, right?" she asked no one. "Only frogs."

A cold shiver ran down her spine as she thought about them.

"I don't know about any two-legged frogs, but if you hang out here long enough, I might show you some pink elephants, Cora said before walking down to a set of customers who took a seat at the other end of the bar.

"I wouldn't mind hanging out here longer," said Tegan. "This is a great feeling, a smaller, more intimate environment. And look at the food on the menu. I could go for a burger," she said.

"Can't you always go for a burger?" asked Kareem.

"I haven't turned down many," Tegan retorted.

Carson finished his pint and picked up the menu to review the foot options. "I could eat," he said, perusing the options. "Plus, the beer is excellent. Some of the best I've had so far on the trip."

"There is an Italian beef on the menu? The foodie in me wants that," Kareem said.

"I'm a foodie too," Tegan replied.

"I'm a foodie. You're like a championship competitive eater," Kareem said to Tegan. "Joey Chestnut's streak might end if he ever encountered you in the contest."

"Whatever. Those Brussel sprouts look amazing, and so does that Heirloom B.L.T.," she said with anticipation.

"I could get down with the fried pickle pesto chicken mac and cheese," said Ty.

"I was thinking something light, but watching the plates go out, that cheeseburger is a two-hander. Grass-fed burger, cheese, add bacon, with a side of fries," said Carson.

Cora returned to take the orders after greeting two elderly men in Bengals gear at the end of the bar.

"On those fries, I recommend either a side of Cheese Wiz, or bump it and top it with melted cheese, pork, scallions, Verde sauce, and red peppers blend," she said, jumping right in.

"Damn, give me the works. It's hard to pass that up," replied Carson.

The food would be helpful in providing the energy to get through a field investigation the next day. A second round of drinks would help with the relaxation necessary to get a good night's rest. Carson placed the order of drinks with Cora. Murklord for Kareem, and Electrify for Ty, a Hazy Mike D for Tegan, and a Bourbon Barrel Heavy Metal Drummer for himself.

As the night concluded, Carson reached into his wallet, dropped some bills on the counter, and waved to Cora.

"Bye, guys. Thanks for coming in!" Cora said as she picked up the glasses and wiped a damp rag across the bar's surface.

"Good luck with your giant frogs!" she called out as the group walked out of the front door.

Carson turned and raised a hand *goodbye* toward her as the door closed. She picked up a business card that had fallen out of Carson's wallet, escaping his notice, and placed it on the edge of the register. The young man sitting alone at the nearby table removed a cellphone from his pocket and made a call.

"Let Commander Williams know the team was here," said the man.

CHAPTER 10

OODA LOOP

The group got an early start to the daytime investigation, driving down Glendale Milford Road heading to the Camp Denison Nature Trail after morning coffee.

"How are we going to get into the area? Chandler said it's private access," asked Ty.

"Chandler texted me he would get there early this morning and leave the access card under a fake rock covering near the access gate. The nature trail has a separate entrance off of Campbell Street, and I don't think we need the card to enter that area, but I want to stop by and pick it up in case. The road to the lake has an access gate where the card will let you in, but in case anyone asks us, we'll have the card on hand. We have to put it back on our way out. He had to be at work early to clean and prep for opening, so he's unable to join us."

"It's good we are getting a look around here early. I don't know if they are animals, or something else. But if they have similar behavior, they are more active in the morning and at night," said Ty.

Stopping by the card reader at the entrance of the lake, Carson opened the door, retrieved the card from under the faux rock, and stepped back inside the vehicle. "That should do it," he said. He backed out onto the road and turned toward the parking lot near the trail entrance.

"This is the location of one of the more recent sightings," said Ty. "If the creatures Chandler saw are the ones we are searching for, hopefully there are still tracks present."

"We are here to observe," reminded Carson. "Hopefully we can find tracks or some other forensic sample, but that's it. If we find something, document it. We don't have the investigative tools to engage the creatures if we encounter them."

Carson parked in the lot off of Campbell, reserved for hikers exploring the trails.

"We're going to start here and not around the lake?" asked Kareem.

"The lake makes sense for frogs," said Carson, "But we're not yet sure what these things are. Maybe they are not frogs?"

"I'm still hoping they are not," added Tegan.

"The eyewitnesses we've talked to so far have reported being near water, but also they were in grassy areas. That's what Parker mentioned. Chandler said they were in a similar area, and even Mango reported seeing them while walking the trails."

A well-traveled dirt path emerged from the end of the driveway, turned a bend, and disappeared into the woods. Tall moss-covered trees, scraggy bushes, and tall grasses obscured the view of the path.

"Let's get it," suggested Carson as he gave his hands a single clap and rubbed them together as if he were working an invisible soap into a hardy lather.

"I enjoy hearing stories about what people have seen," stated Ty, "But there is nothing like a field investigation where we take that information and search for ourselves."

The sunny morning was a little less light with each step deeper down the wooded trail. Tegan looked at each shrub, bush, and tree as they followed the trail, searching for clues. Carson noticed her reaction to each moving branch or the sound of the wind through the tall grasses. She noticed many small rocks, painted solid colors with cheerful messages and designs on top. People placed the rocks along the edge of trail, the base of a tree, and even a few added inside random openings in some trees.

"It seems to be a well-traveled trail, based on the number of rocks resembling offerings and the dirt surfacing through the grass on the trail," Tegan said.

"The grass is worn down," noted Kareem.

"Good observations. Keep searching the area. Maybe we can find skin, hair, or some footprints," said Carson.

"Some of those historical sightings attributed to the Loveland Frog mentioned leathery skin, but also matted hair on its body that made it look textured," reminded Ty.

"We also have to adjust our line of sight because we can't only look for signs of four feet tall bipedal creatures. Remember, they can crouch down like an actual frog as well," said Kareem.

"If we spot them, most reports suggest they will run away," replied Ty.

"Or use that device people say emits a bright light, then escape," added Carson.

"Remember it tried to attack Vivian," stated Tegan. "Maybe it is because she's a woman? Or maybe she was too close?"

"That's possible. All the other tips we have received have been from men," recalled Carson.

"And the historical reports were also all male," stated Ty.

"Also, there always seem to be at least three, maybe four of them," said Kareem.

"That could come into play when we locate them," pondered Carson. "Each of our prior investigations has been solo creatures. This is the first time we are up against a group of unknowns."

"A group of frogs is called an army," said Tegan. "Hopefully they don't act like an army!"

"I am getting a weird feeling," replied Kareem. "It's pretty eerie out here, even in the daytime. We've got this little tributary with water running here, but even though there's a city nearby, this spot is quiet and a little creepy," he observed.

"If we were out here to fish, it wouldn't be creepy, but since we are searching for some unknown creature that is hidden and may or may not be dangerous, our senses are on full alert, making it have more of a suspenseful feeling," stated Ty.

Carson turned his body in each direction, swiveling his head when he did, attempting to orient himself with the area.

"Looks like the lake is down this path," Carson said, looking left. "The river is off to the right, so I assume this path heads to it," he said, pointing to the right.

Continuing to stare at both options, he noticed the trail that disappeared to the left was dirt with brief spots of grass remaining. A path bending to the right was lesser worn.

"Which way?" asked Carson.

"Robert Frost directs us to take the lesser-worn path. Can't go wrong listening to his beautiful words," said Kareem. "Plus, the right will be more secluded based on the height of the grass compared to the left. Animals like seclusion, and if they are intelligent beings?

"They will go out of their way not to be noticed," said Ty.

"With less foot traffic comes less damage to the recovery sights of potential physical evidence," said Kareem.

The temperature felt cooler under the canopy of the trees. Fallen leaves covered the trail, crunching under the feet of the investigators as they continued down the undisturbed path.

Thirty yards ahead, a small alcove in the path jutted out from a small grove of trees.

"Look at that clearing ahead," signaled Carson. "Somewhat obscured from sight, but noticeable from the main trail if, one is looking that way. Chandler could have seen movement from the fork in the road, drawing his eyes down this path," he suggested.

"It would otherwise be unnoticeable unless there was something that would cause him to look down here," suggested Ty.

"Let's check it out," said Kareem.

The group moved closer to the spot. The guys were more anxious than Tegan.

"The leaves here have been disturbed," revealed Carson as they got closer.

"You're right! And look, the ground has also been torn up," said Kareem. "Right at the base of these small trees."

"Something scraped these evergreens up near the base," pointed out Tegan

"My guess is it was scratched by animals. Perhaps deer rutting? This time of year is near deer season and there is an increase in buck activity," said Kareem.

"That's a good point," stated Carson. "I used to go hunting with my dad and the males not only scrape trees, but dug shallow pits where they urinate and rolled around to make mud that they coat themselves in. They use tree trunks and branches to rub their antlers and remove the velvet."

Ty walked around the area above the scratched trees. "Look, here's a small pit here that's muddy and hallowed out. This is a sign of a deer rut."

"But this side of the tree looks different. It's not a muddy pit large enough for a deer, but looks like a small dig site," said Kareem.

Tegan bent down to get a closer look at the upturned soil.

"I see nothing suspicious. Some dirt, some gravel, a few rocks."

Kareem picked up a dirt-covered rock and rubbed it with his thumb and index finger. "Looks like there's some color to it," he said. "Kind of mottled green and pink appearance.

"That looks like unakite," replied Tegan.

"What's that?" asked Carson.

"It's a crystal stone that I saw in the occult shop in Phoenix. It's used in metaphysical practices and meditation to inspire a sense of urgency as you realize how time slips through your fingers. It's a stone of clarity that increases your sense of being in the now," she said.

"Maybe that's what these things were after? They were digging for unakite but were scared off when Chandler got too close?" theorized Carson.

"What would these frog-like creatures want with a shiny rock?" asked Ty. "And there seems to be a small deposit there. If they were interested in them, why leave these others?"

"From what we know about these things, I think it is time we accept they are not frogs, but some advanced being. We know primates can use tools, but I haven't seen other species capable. It makes me think they are something different we haven't seen before," suggested Carson. "They left some behind because they were interrupted, but why do they want the mineral? I don't know."

The group fanned out to explore the area for more clues.

To the right of the path, the banks sloped down a hill and lead to the edge of the Little Miami River. Tegan kicked the leaves with her foot, overturning a translucent white stone.

"This looks like a piece of selenite," she said. "They used this in the shop to represent spiritual purity, light, and connection to the angelic realms."

"Likely means there are some gypsum caves around here," reported Ty. "Maybe a hidden entrance near the river somewhere."

"We know the Mammoth Cave system isn't too far away down in Kentucky has some Gypsum Flower formations in dry parts of the cave. It's thought they result from carbon dioxide and sulfur combining during cave's formation," replied Carson.

"Over here!" Kareem shouted as he spotted a group of prints in the soft, exposed dirt. "Looks like footprints with five toes each, but it also looks webbed."

"They are around the base of these pine trees and all along this ridge before the bank slopes down," replied Tegan.

"There's some deer tracks here too, which explains the trees being cut up like we thought," said Carson. "Those other tracks seem like frogs, but much larger than a typical frog."

"Makes sense. If these creatures are about four feet tall and fifty to seventy-five pounds, they would have enormous feet. By the looks of it, our guys were here," said Ty.

Carson turned, scanning the landscape for more clues.

"I think you're right," said Carson. "The number of tracks suggests there were multiple similar creatures here. I think we're on the right track. They were here and digging for this unakite before Chandler happened along and they escaped down the hill and to the river," he said.

"But why would a giant frog need a metaphysical stone used in meditation?" asked Tegan.

Kareem continued to search the ground for clues, finding nothing more than another handful of gravel obscuring a four-inch-long dirty rock with a glimpse of purple. Kareem picked it up and rubbed more of the dirt off it, revealing the stone's deep purple coloring.

"Not sure what this is, but I dig the color," Kareem said, rubbing it until all the dirt was off. He stared at it for a few seconds before deciding to put it in his pocket.

"It's getting cooler out here, and I think it's obvious they are no longer here," said Carson. "Whatcha say we return the access card to the gated entrance and get out of here. Maybe get a drink and go over our plans?"

An hour later, the group was sitting at a four-person wooden table inside Little Miami Brewing Company, where Ida Fawcett took their drink orders.

"It was good to get out there today and explore the grounds of a recent sighting," said Carson. "But now we have to decide the next steps. We could write it off as deer activity with the damage to the trees. Even the upturned ground could be a sign of deer pawing or digging depressions in the ground," he said. "We saw evidence of digging to make a mud pit."

"The deer population is active right now, so maybe that makes sense," said Ty. "Chandler said he saw these creatures at the Preserve. The clues we found could be deer, but not the tracks. That's the only thing we found that suggests something unknown was there."

"Is it worth pursuing? The evidence we saw was minimal in suggesting unknown creatures were in the area. Without those tracks, it would have been a disappointing investigation. As it is, I think we have more questions," said Kareem.

"The tracks were around those loose stones. Gravel makes sense because it used to be an excavation site. The unakite may be a coincidence," suggested Tegan.

"We found the selenite in the area and this unknown purple stone," added Kareem.

"You said the selenite comes from Gypsum formations in a cave," Carson said to Ty. "Vivian spotted them in the subway, which is like a cave," he continued. "Maybe there is a connection there? Maybe these are subterranean creatures?"

"Subterranean would mean they live in darkness, which, if you think about all the sightings, even going back to the 1950s. The sightings occurred at night, or in the dark, as you mentioned with Vivian's experience," said Ty.

"Except for the first story where the college student saw them along the river and our boy, Mango," reminded Kareem.

"Yes, those two seem to be outliers," said Carson.

"When were those sightings?" asked Tegan, looking at her phone. "Mango was late last week and the first sighting a couple weeks before, a few days before my birthday, if I recall," said Carson.

"Looking at the local weather the week before your birthday, it was heavy rains most of the week," said Tegan. "And there was rain earlier this week as well. Maybe both sightings occurred when it was overcast and raining," she theorized.

"You're right. Our witnesses said they had a heavy storm here," replied Ty.

Ida returned with the drinks: a Pterodactyl Hefeweizen for Carson, Peace Frog IPA for Kareem, the Statesman Belgian Strong Golden Ale, and Wang Dang Doodle sour fruited beer for Tegan.

"I'm no animal behaviorist," said Ty, "but we've been out in the woods hunting creatures, both known and unknown for years. Many animals are more active as a storm nears. Especially getting closer to late autumn and early winter, they might take the time to prepare for the changes in season. A dark and dreary time might be the right time to get out and prepare. They wouldn't have to worry about the heat of the sun beating them down."

"The thing that stands out to me is not only the size in the description of the creatures, but their use of tools and that instrument," said Kareem. "Yes, some animals have been observed using tools, but not tools like shovels or axes, and the want that emits light? That's technology, and a technology we don't understand. It sounds like an advanced species. And I'm not saying it was aliens, but after what we saw in Phoenix,

I think it was aliens," concluded Kareem.

"Aliens? Seems farfetched," suggested Ty.

"How else would you explain it? The description of these creatures does not fit any earthly thing we know. They use a lighted instrument to help escape, and we found a folder labeled Loveland in that underground facility in Phoenix. We know there were aliens there, and the government seemed to know something strange was happening in Ohio," Kareem calculated.

"And with all the sightings being night, underground, or cloudy, maybe that suggests they are not used to Earth's sun," interjected Tegan.

"One thing is certain. We have to get back out there and do another investigation. Using what we're piecing together now, I think we have to do it at night," said Carson.

"Agreed," said Ty. "I think we move a little upstream near Adams Road. That's close to the Branch Hill area where the first Frogman sighting occurred. Another sighting occurred at the Loveland-Madeira Corridor, and we have Mango's sighting. They're all close," said Ty.

"That's also near to where Björn spotted them on the near the river and the paranormal team encountered them at the castle," added Tegan.

"Tomorrow it's time to act," said Carson. "Ty, do you have any contacts here in town that could help us out?"

"Yes, I think I have the guy," Ty replied, searching his phone for the contact he was thinking about. "Got it. I'll call him and set something up for tomorrow morning," Ty said.

"Okay, call him and see if we can't work out a trap. Maybe we can get lucky and capture one of these guys and then we can figure out what they want and why they are here," said Carson.

"From Phoenix we know aliens not only exist, but they have been to Earth already," said Kareem. "There could be thousands of different aliens. They don't have to resemble grays or E.T. Maybe there are species that look like larger versions of our frogs," he said.

"What would an extraterrestrial frog want from Earth? Specifically, southwestern Ohio?" asked Carson.

"In Hollywood, it is always a dark reason: destroying Earth, harvesting humans for food or breeding, draining our oceans, or something like that," said Tegan.

"Maybe they are here to scout out a new home? Perhaps there is something wrong with theirs and they need to find an alternative? Suggested Ty.

"Or instead of finding a new home, maybe they are repairing theirs? Perhaps Earth has some raw material that they could extract and return to their home planet?" added Carson.

"But why here? There are hundreds, if not millions, of rocky extrasolar planets around the galaxy that scientists have discovered," said Teagan.

"Yes, but Earth is unique. Terrestrial planets might be common, but Earth is the only one that we know of with atmosphere and plate tectonics that keep our climate stable. The plates shift and make Earth a dynamic environment with moving pieces that slide, rub, and crunch alongside each other and churn out new crusts and minerals," said Carson.

"The key to answering these questions is to come face-to-face with them, watch their behavior, and see if we can capture one," said Ty.

"After Phoenix, aliens are as frightening to me as frogs," said Tegan. "If we can capture them and get them off of the street, that's something I can drink to," she said, hoisting her drink in the air.

CHAPTER 11

BIG FROG IN A SMALL POND

Sitting at a white plastic booth in the Bagel Bandit Breakfast Joint, Ty sat waiting on Lemmy Jenkins to arrive. Sipping an Espresso con panna, he starred at his phone, looking for more news on sightings of the Loveland Frogman, er Frogmen, as they appear to be dealing with. He looked up after hearing the bell hanging around the door's handle jingle.

Lemmy Jenkins was a forty-two-year-old high school shop teacher who enjoys working on cars, attending museums, and reading. An intelligent and reliable man, his chief interest was cryptozoology and building traps designed to capture unknown animals. Ty met him two years ago after a speaking engagement in Louisville, where Ty discussed T.I.M.E.'s experience with hunting the chupacabra. While talking about how they trapped the creature, it triggered the attention of one man in attendance. Lemmy Jenkins. After the presentation, Ty stuck around for a Q&A session where Lemmy told Ty about his interest in cryptozoology and his expertise with building traps. The two men exchanged numbers, and as luck would have it, Lemmy was a Cincinnati native.

"Glad to hear from you, Ty," said Lemmy. "It's been a while."

"About a couple of years, isn't it?"

"'Bout that."

"We are in Ohio, and we could use someone with your skills," Ty said.

"What are you fellas up against this time?" Lemmy asked.

"We're investigating the Loveland Frog."

"I've heard tales growing up around here. Never seen it myself, but I have attempted to search for it a time or two," Lemmy replied.

"We haven't spotted it ourselves yet either, but we've had several recent sightings," Ty responded. "And it's not an 'it', but a 'they'," he said.

"They?"

"All the people we have talked to the past few days report three beings. They are always together and seem to communicate with each other and searching for something. They can use tools and seem to be intelligent beings," Ty reported.

"From what I know, most accounts I read mentioned holding some kind of wand. I don't know if it's a weapon or something else," added Lemmy.

"Our sources seem to think it is something else. These creatures don't often attack humans. Prior sightings report they run away when people get close, but there have been a couple of instances. One woman we talked to spotted them in a subway station and said they came after her," continued Ty. "We think maybe the wand emits a light that temporarily blinds the victim, allowing the creatures to run away."

"What else do you know about these creatures?" asked Lemmy.

"All the reports we have received have the creature close to water, the Little Miami River, to be exact. People also see mostly them at night or on overcast days. We explored a location where they were observed to be digging for something. We saw evidence of a small dig site and some scattered rocks. The rocks were unakite, and we think that's what they were trying to find. That's the only thing we found in that area, except for a couple of other loose stones," Ty stated.

"If I remember correctly, these things are about four feet tall and over fifty pounds," recalled Lemmy.

"That's what we've heard from the witnesses," replied Ty.

"I'm thinking of a falling-cage trap with a triggered floor," said Lemmy. "We find a good open area to set the trap. It's got a floor that we'll cover with a bit of dirt or mulch. Bury some of those rocks in the dirt and leave a couple near the surface. We have a raised box trap above, and when the frogmen dig to get the stones, their shovel will trigger the mechanism under the mulch, causing the trap to fall on them. The box itself will have small bamboo bars on each side, spaced only three inches apart. That will them so they cannot escape," suggested Lemmy.

"For something off the top of your head without visiting the site, that's sounds magnificent! How long will it take to construct something like that?" asked Ty.

"A few hours. I have a large concentration of bamboo growing close to me. That's the most time-consuming part. I have the rest of the materials at my workshop. But those rocks, I don't know where to get those," Lemmy stated.

"I can order those for you at a new age shop. I'll send you the address if you can pick it up on the way," Ty stated.

"Where are you going to want the trap?"

"We were planning around Adams Road near Ertel Run," answered Ty.

"Alrighty, guess I will get to work and see you out there this afternoon. There's some good, heavy tree cover around some of the houses right there. Should work well to hide the trap. We can camouflage it real good with leaf covering," said Lemmy.

"Sounds good. I'll Venmo you the money now and text you our location when we get out there later," said Ty.

"Glad to help," Lemmy said.

The two men stood and exchanged a hardy handshake, before walking out together.

Inside Cartridge Brewing, the rest of the T.I.M.E. team was sitting at a large granite-top table. They constructed this brewery on the banks of the Little Miami River, in 1916 as the home to the Peters Cartridge Factory. Now renovated into a fifteen-barrel brewhouse, the brewery opened in the fall of 2020 and serves once again as a gathering place for the Kings Mills and surrounding communities.

"I wonder how Ty is making out with finding a trap?" asked Tegan.

"I don't know, but hopefully he's on his way. I ordered him this Smokestack," replied Carson. "It's rare to see a smoked beer on the menu, so I figured that'd be the one he wanted.

"I was happy to find this tart Hollow Point Hibiscus Ale," replied Tegan.

"This Sabot IPA is something else as well. Big flavor with a lot of hops, but a nice clean malt base," added Kareem.

"We might have to order lunch too and kill some time. We've got our nighttime investigation tonight and we need to have the energy to get after these creatures," stated Carson. "Speaking of big flavor, this Opening Salvo Imperial IPA is a great dry-hopped beer. I might combine that with the pulled pork sandwich."

Ty entered the brewery and looked for his friends, locating them at the large table. "Hey, guys. We're set for this afternoon," Ty reported.

"That's great! I am eager to get back out there and put more pieces of this puzzle together," said Carson.

"Hopefully we can capture them tonight and put an end to this mystery," said Kareem.

"I'm all for that," announced Tegan. "Sooner we're done, the better."

"We were thinking of also putting in an order for food," Carson said to Ty. "I got you a beer," he said, sliding the glass over to his friend.

"I told Lemmy everything we know about these Frogmen," said Ty. "He was familiar with them, at least reputation-wise. He was born and raised in the area and grew up hearing about them. He's a cryptid fan himself, likely because of the stories he heard growing up."

"It's good to have someone who doesn't freak out when we talk about hunting monsters," Kareem said. "At least that won't be weird for him."

"Right up his alley," answered Ty. "He has some friends who are also investigators, and he's going to get some equipment for us, including a couple of thermals and a parabolic mic."

"Things are shaping up for us and this night investigation," said Carson. "We will be ready to jump right in tonight."

"Until then, I think I'm going to jump into that rib sandwich on the menu," said Ty.

"Amateur," teased Tegan.

"What are you ordering?" asked Ty.

"Full rack of ribs. Go big or go home," answered Tegan.

Kareem's eyes grew large. "Well, someone brought their appetite," he snarked.

"A girl's gotta eat," she responded.

"Sweet potato quinoa burger for me," Kareem said, laying the menu back on the countertop.

Late afternoon arrived as the sun neared the horizon around 5:00 p.m. The gang stood along a gravel driveway off Adams Road awaiting Lemmy. Ty's phone lit up and vibrated, signaling his friend wasn't far away.

"Hopefully this trap doesn't weigh too much. It's bamboo," Ty answered.

"With four of us, we should be able to carry it," stated Kareem.

"I can carry the thermals," said Tegan.

"I thought that rack of ribs would help you carry the trap," responded Kareem.

"Nah, you guys got this," she said.

A black pickup with an attached trailer arrived and pulled to the side of the road in front of them.

"Special delivery!" yelled Lemmy.

"Man, that thing looks great!" said Carson, looking at the trap resting on the trailer.

"It should do the job," replied Lemmy. "These bars I could get a little closer than three inches apart, so they won't be able to escape through them. We will have to construct the floor and trigger mechanism on site, but that won't take no time. I figure if we can find a spot on the trail that's close to the river, it will attract them. The cage will be hanging above and, with the tree cover, should blend right in. We can dig up some loose dirt and I got a couple bags of pine bark mulch to throw down. I picked up them fancy rocks to add. If that's what they're after, they will find them. Once they dig, the trap will fall, capturing them inside," Lemmy explained.

"Yes! That's what I'm talking about!" said Carson. "I'm eager to see it in action."

The neighborhood contained many sub-divided housing plots with thick tree covering above the dirt trail that followed the bank of the tributary Ertel Run. A short distance away was the Little Miami River, cutting its way through the trees and luxury housing development on both sides. The guys carried the trap down the trail, placing it in a small clearing at the edge of the trees.

"This spot will work fine," Lemmy stated. "Off the side of the trail, close to the water, but secluded enough anyone walking the trail wouldn't notice. Let's push these leaves away and install the flooring. We'll cover it back up with leaves, dirt, and mulch, and then set the trigger."

Carson, Kareem, and Tegan worked on clearing the ground while Ty and Lemmy raised the bamboo trap into the air. Lemmy tied the trap with a large rope and began work on the floor as the last remnants of daylight faded. A few minutes later, he declared the trap complete and ready to set. Lemmy's handiwork met the team's approval, and they were eager to get started. At least most of them were.

"That should do it," Lemmy declared. "Ya'll have fun and be safe out here. I'm going to skedaddle back to the house and catch up on the basketball scores. We'll reach out tomorrow and see what you caught."

An hour later, the group was ready to explore the trails. The temperature dropped after sunset and a slight breeze kicked up.

"Let's stick together," said Carson as he took the point and navigated the worn grass path through the trees. The darkness intensified as they entered a wooded segment of the trail. The woods seemed typical tonight: the sound of the normal nighttime melody of frogs along the water line, crickets, grasshoppers, and cicadas singing out in a nocturnal chorus, while the song of the katydids reflected the seasonal change *katydid, katydidn't* that signaled an oncoming frost was imminent. The group of human visitors crept deeper into the woods. The insects' music dampened as the visitors grew too close to their hiding area on, around, and underneath their protective leaves.

"Good little ways in here, isn't it?" says Carson as they head deeper into the woods.

"I can't see how that Mango guy walked through these dense woods. Hopefully it opens a little more ahead," said Ty.

"What's that?"

"That guy you met in the bathroom. Mango… This area here isn't too far from where he said he was hunting for mushrooms and saw the Frogmen," said Ty.

"Damn, you're right!" said Carson. "I remember he said Ertel Run, but I didn't connect the two until I began looking at this map," he said, looking at his phone. "It didn't click that run was a creek. Adam's Road crosses over the creek here and this entire area is a simple walk for someone like Mango who is used to the woods like the back of his hand."

"It's difficult to see anything out in these woods," said Kareem.

"After going over the eyewitness accounts and not finding any signs of them yesterday, we had to switch it up. These creatures run at night, that's why we're here at night," said Carson.

Tegan walked at the back of the pack, directing the parabolic mic in each direction as they walked.

"These insects are super loud through these headphones," said reported.

Kareem held a thermal device, scanning the tree line for signs of life.

"Anything yet?" asked Carson while Kareem continued scanning the area.

"Damn, nothing yet," reported Kareem.

"Let's continue pushing up this trail," suggested Carson.

"Remember where the trap is set and if we see anything, try to push them that way," added Ty.

"Keep an eye out for other animals. There's hopefully more than abnormally large bipedal frogs out here. When darkness takes over, the forest becomes inhabited by strange and fascinating wildlife," said Carson.

"That's what I am afraid of," said Tegan.

"What's wrong? Normally you aren't this nervous on these nighttime investigations," replied Kareem.

"I know. I'm uneasy about this, and I don't know why. Probably because they look like frogs and they are the snakes to my Indiana Jones," Tegan admitted before pausing and focusing on listening. She heard a rustle in the leaves and the snap of a branch. "I'm picking something up on the mic," she said.

"Where?" Kareem asked as he spun around, aiming at the thermal in the general area.

A small red and orange figure emerged on the device's screen.

"I'm seeing it!" Kareem whispered.

Taking a few steps closer, the creature's thermal image raised its head, looking at Kareem atop a fallen log.

"It's up ahead," he whispered.

Ty shone a military-grade flashlight in the direction. The beast turned its head and coiled back as the light hit its face, causing its eyes to reflect yellow. Bathed in light, the crew could see what they were dealing with.

"Raccoon," let's keep moving said Ty.

"If I remember the map correctly, we can follow the Run south to the Little Miami River," said Carson. "The next road down is Loveland Road, where some of the original sightings occurred. The Loveland Castle where the Porkopolis team spotted the creatures is to the west. Less than a mile as the crow flies."

"I think this area is a hot spot for activity. All the sightings are within a five-mile radius of here," added Ty.

As they continued walked south along the trail, Kareem kept panning the area with the thermal. The nighttime sounds of insects and amphibians were now quiet. Tegan paused at the increased silence.

"It's eerily quiet now, and it doesn't seem to be those insects close to us, but the entire woods in this area," she stated.

"Hey guys, I'm getting something on thermal," Kareem announced. "Looks like two figures showing purple, blue, and black on the display," he said.

"The darker colors represent cooler objects that produce less infrared and heat wavelengths," replied Carson.

"Frogs and toads are cold-blooded, so their body temperatures take on the temperature of the surrounding environment," added Ty. "This time of night even the warm rocks temperature has faded, giving less attraction to using them to warm their bodies."

"Guys," Kareem said, "these two stood up."

"What?" asked Carson.

"There were crouched down low to the ground, but now they have stood up on their hind legs," Kareem clarified. "Definitely something up there!"

Carson took a few steps but couldn't make anything out.

"Here, check it out," Kareem said, handing the thermal camera to Carson. Carson panned the area as the others attempted to see what was up ahead. Ty turned toward where Kareem stopped the thermal images.

"See anything, Ty?" asked Carson.

"I don't see a thing," he answered.

The images reappeared on the thermal display. There were now three distinct images.

"Right behind ya. You might see nothing, but you've got something leering over your shoulder, brother," replied Carson.

Ty turned around, and shined his flashlight in that direction, but there was nothing there.

"Sounds like something running away," Tegan said, listening to the mic through her headphones.

"Let's move hard straight ahead and see if we can spot them again," suggested Carson.

"I think those were our guys," said Kareem. "Three images, cold-bodied, and we saw it stand up."

"Like Ray Shockey, Jr. saw in 1972," said Carson.

"And in this general area," added Ty.

They continued to walk briskly ahead, panning the thermal device, the mic, and the flashlight as they went, hoping to stumble upon the mysterious creatures once again. Eighty feet ahead, they stopped at the base of a couple of trees where the flashlight revealed the trunk had severe damage.

"I think this is where they were when we spotted them on thermal," said Tegan.

"These trees are all beat to hell," said Carson. "Why would they damage the tree?"

"Remember yesterday where we spotted the dig site? There was a tree that was scratched up also. We thought it was from a buck, but maybe it was the Frogmen?" said Tegan.

"What kind of tree is it?" asked Kareem.

Ty walked over to a low-hanging branch and opened an app on his phone. Taking a photo of the leaves, he looked down at the phone's display.

The leaves were seven inches long and three inches broad that hung down from the branches and contained about ten lobed white petals and open dense panicles ten inches long. Some displayed a smooth, dry oblong fruit.

"Says it's a *Styrax platanifolius*," read Ty. "The family grows in eastern and southeastern Asia, but this specific species is native to Texas, Northeast Mexico, and parts of the Midwest. The family Styrax contains about a hundred thirty different species," said Ty.

"Does it have any special uses? Why would these frog men damage a tree?" asked Kareem.

"There is a resin produced from the bark and sap of the tree called Benzoin resin. Apparently, there are records of international trade of the resin back to the late Middle Ages," stated Ty. "They have used Storax resin in perfumes, certain types of incense, and medicines. It says its uses range from air freshener to incense to medical uses as a disinfectant and local anesthetic to a restorative dental material to cosmetics," he concluded.

"It still seems like that doesn't connect with these creatures," said Carson. "What would they need with those properties?"

"The sighting Vivian had still puzzles me," said Tegan. "If it attracted these creatures to the storax trees, maybe that works for all other witness accounts because they were outdoors – but Vivian was indoors. There are no trees inside the subway."

"Look around through these leaves. Maybe the tree isn't the connection. I think it still is the unakite. If they were here around the trees, maybe they were looking for the rock and left some behind," suggested Carson.

Tegan and Ty ran the palm of their hands face down along the ground, pushing fallen leaves out of the way. The ground didn't display any signs of digging, but Carson theorized perhaps it was because the group walked up on the beings before they had the chance to start. Ty's hand ran over a partial buried rock that caused him to stop and dig out. Rubbing the dirt from the rock's surface, he tossed it back to the ground. "I don't see any unakite here. This little purple rock is the only thing I found," he said.

"Purple rock? Which one?" asked Kareem.

Ty pointed to the general direction he tossed the rock was, causing Kareem to scout the area to reclaim it.

"This is like the rock I found yesterday. I haven't seen this type of rock before, but I liked the color, so I kept it. Once they I rubbed the dirt off, it's a cool rock. I bet it's intensified if polished," Kareem stated.

"We've seen these trees in both locations, but not utekite. However, this unknown rock is at both locations. Coincidence?" asked Carson.

The group searched the area for another ninety minutes but found no additional signs of the creatures.

"I think the well has run dry," said Carson. "Maybe we should call it a night?"

"I think you're right. If those things on the thermal were the frogmen, I think we scared them off. They won't come back here tonight," said Ty.

"There's still time for a nightcap," Kareem said, looking at his watch.

"Might as well," suggested Tegan. "It will give us time to reflect and maybe regroup tomorrow."

Three miles away, the group walked into the doors of Dizzy Beaver Beer Garden and Grill. The *Grill* was an important word in the name, allowing it, as a restaurant, to remain open until 2:30 a.m. rather than the typical 11 p.m. restriction faced by brewery-only venues. This time of day, the bar was empty, reserved for those who were escaping the pressures of the day. Pressures of life that, for most people, seemed to increase over the past several months. Carson remembered those pressures he faced only a few years ago and the frequent late nights and early mornings he used to escape, or rather hide from, at Giddy Ups. These used to be his people.

He didn't have those same pressures today. Overall, life was good. The cryptid investigations that began as an almost accidental re-entry into an old favorite pastime had now turned into a full-time job. His coworkers were his best friends, and they enjoyed craft beer, investigating hidden animals, and speaking as experts in the field at colleges, universities, and lecture halls around the country. He paid his bills on time, money was coming in, and people sought him out, eager to see him.

Now the pressures faced were work- related. It was difficult finding enough time to investigate the rising number of cases submitted to the T.I.M.E. Agency or the pressure of solving an investigation. These critical steps helped the scientific world identify hidden animals and bring them to the forefront of the known world. Knowing their investigations and field notes contributed to the body of knowledge and helped communities that felt like they were in danger was a great feeling. Families could sleep better at night knowing they and their families were safe.

As Carson continued to reflect on the changes in his life, the team took a seat at the bar. Carson caught up and looked at the chalkboard menu on the wall behind the bar. Gene Jefferson, working behind the bar tonight, walked over to take their order.

"So many options on this menu. I don't know what to pick! I guess I'll go with the number eighteen," said Carson.

"Is this the number that rings to you?" inquired Gene.

"Yeah, I guess so. For starters anyway," replied Carson.

Gene turned toward the bar handles to pour the first drink, turning his head over his left shoulder he called out, "Let me know if the rest of you are ready yet."

"I think I will have the Mt. Carmel Hibiscus Blueberry Blonde," Tegan said. "This sounds like a saison, but I liked that tart hibiscus the other day."

"Here's your Highgrain Isar Weiss," Gene said with a wink, sitting the drink down on a coaster in front of Carson.

"Moerlein Barbarossa for me," said Ty.

"Hofbrauhaus Dunkel," added Kareem.

"Good choice. That one was voted as number one beer in Cincinnati in a recent poll," reported Gene.

"Momma always said I had good taste," replied Kareem.

Kareem reached into his pocket and emptied the contents on the bar: His hotel room keycard, his wallet, the phone, and the purple rock from the woods. He picked up the rock and rubbed it with his fingers, a relaxation attempt to bring his emotions down. They were always heightened during, and after, an investigation. The motion drew the attention of a woman sitting kitty-corner of him on the side of the bar.

"I don't know about you guys, but what we've seen so far and the clues we have found seem all cattywampus," Kareem said. "We've stumbled onto some things, but it feels they are not lined up correctly."

"Excuse me, sorry for eavesdropping," said Emily Pickles, a woman in her mid-thirties with piercing brown eyes and mid-back length, curly, mousey brown hair pulled into a bun. Even from a few feet away Kareem noticed an aroma of dank weed and sweet milk chocolate. "I noticed that rock you have. Where did you get it?" she asked.

"Oh this?" Kareem said, looking at the stone in his hands. "Found it in the woods. Not sure what it is, but I liked the color," he said.

Emily got up from her seat on the side of the bar and moved to an empty seat beside Kareem.

"I'm Emily," she said.

"Nice to meet you, Emily."

"I'm also a geologist. I am surprised to see such a rare mineral," she said as Kareem placed the rock down on the bar top. "Do you mind?" she asked.

Shaking his head, Emily picked up the stone and held it close to her eye.

"This is called treenbergite. It's a rare mineral and if we can remove more of this dirt…" she said, dipping her napkin in a water glass and wiping the stone clean, "you can see sparkles."

"Wow, it's even better than I imagined," replied Kareem. "It thought it was just a purple rock."

"The crystal structure of treenbergite is unique and a one-of-a-kind mineral in its class, mostly because of its rare hexagonal crystallization. I only know of a few places around the planet where scientists have located these rocks," Emily added.

"What's it used for?" asked Kareem. "We found it in the woods near the Little Miami River. It was close to some trees that some creature we are looking for had damaged," he explained.

"Now I'm even more intrigued! A creature?"

"Never got a light on him," said Ty. "But we saw they can run fast."

"They?" repeated Emily.

"Yes, there were three of them. Have you heard of the Loveland Frog? Asked Carson.

"I've heard talk, but I counted it as local urban legends, and nothing more," said Emily.

"We think they are more than legend. We have several eyewitnesses, and we saw them ourselves tonight," added Carson.

"From a distance. On thermal cam," clarified Tegan.

"And you think these frogmen are connected to the Treenbergite?" asked Emily.

"That's what we're not sure about. We found piece of this mineral and two different locations where the creatures were spotted. Both locations also had trees that were cut up," Kareem said. "Ty, what kind of tree was it?"

"Styrax platanifolius," he replied.

"We found it has a resin in it that is used for medical and cosmetic uses. I don't know if there is a connection there to the mineral. The only other things we found were small pieces of utekite and selenite, but only at one site."

"Interesting combination of minerals. The selenite could come from a nearby cave, specifically a gypsum cave. A gypsum cave is a natural karstic formation in gypsum. Sinkholes are the major hazard associated with karst landforms in Ohio, and there are thousands of them in the state. It's not limited to sinkholes - other solutional features, such as caves, springs, disappearing streams, and enlarged fractures, are known as karst terrains," Emily said.

As they continued talking, Carson interrupted to ask about another round. "One more? What about you Emily?"

"I'm down for one more," replied Kareem, again picking up the menu and sharing with Emily.

"What do you like to drink, Emily?" asked Kareem.

"I'm a pale ale/IPA girl myself," she said.

"Me too," he said with a smile.

"I'm going a little lighter. It's late for me," Emily said. "Vanilla Cream."

"Punch you in the eyePA for me," said Kareem.

"What's next for you?" asked Gene.

"Let me get the Doom Petal," Carson said.

"Full pours? We can do five, ten, or sixteen ounces," replied Gene.

"Last call? Let's go sixteen," Carson said.

"Backbeat Coffee Blonde," said Tegan.

"And for me… Roebling Vanilla Espresso Porter, said Ty.

"At least we can put a name to this rock," said Kareem. "Still a lot of pieces that are up in the air. What is it used for? Is that what the frogmen are after? Or is it the tree?

"I read up more on the tree we found, and they briefly described the resin in an article. It said Benzoin is the sap that comes from cuts in the trunk of trees that belong to the Styrax family. In addition, both trees we found had cuts in the trunks. We know these creatures were at both locations and we found disfigured trees and this treenbergite at each site. We have found other things, but the only three things that are constant are the frogmen, benzoin, and treenbergite," stated Ty.

"There is a connection there," said Emily. "I know nothing about frogmen, but benzoin is an indicator of treenbergite. As I mentioned, it's a rare mineral, and we are still learning about not only its purposes, but also its properties, and where it is located. One theory is that where there is benzoin, there is an increased chance treenbergite is nearby," Emily said.

"How rare is this mineral?" asked Tegan.

"They have found it in a few locations on the planet, near water. I know for sure they have found it in deposits in Goshen, Indiana near the Elkhart River, the Egyptian Nile, and South Kensington, Middlesex," Emily stated.

"And Loveland near the Little Miami River," added Ty.

"Apparently," returned Emily.

"Goshen, Indiana…." Carson started. "That sounds familiar to me," he said as he took a sip of Doom Petal.

"We haven't been there to investigate anything," replied Tegan.

"No, but… there was a story about an incident in the Elkhart River in either the 50s or 60s where a woman who was swimming with a friend reported being grabbed by something unknown in the river. Remember the one Buck told us?" Carson asked.

"Now that you mention it, yes! Late 50s I believe it was. The public dismissed it because she said she caught a glimpse from the corner of her eye of the animal. Her description sounded similar to the *Creature from the Black Lagoon*, and that movie came out in 1954," said Ty.

"But that's not uncommon for the public to dismiss something away. It happened the same way with the original chupacabra sightings in Puerto Rico after the movie Species came out. But we found that to be real, didn't we?" Carson asked. "If you didn't know what it was you might describe it like a movie creature, especially one that was popular. When the *Creature from the Black Lagoon* came out, it was an original concept and widely viewed. It might not be the same, but that description it could give a general description most people would understand," Carson stated. "Another thing that struck my mind," said Kareem. "Emily, you mentioned South Kensington."

"Yes, in England. They have found there Treenbergite," Emily stated.

"Also from South Kensington is Sunray Gardens where Beatrix Potter grew up," Kareem said.

"Okay, you've secured your spot at the Celis Brewery trivia table when we get back to Austin," stated Carson.

"Beatrix Potter wrote *Peter Rabbit*?" Tegan said as a statement that sounded more like a question.

"Yes, *The Tale of Peter Rabbit*, *The Tale of Jemima Puddle-Duck*, *The Tale of Squirrel Nutkin*, and of importance to our situation, *The Tale of Mr. Jeremy Fisher*," said Kareem.

"I'm down with Peter Rabbit, but I don't know those other books," said Ty.

"Jeremy Fisher is a frog. A frog who catches worms, fishes for minnows, is bipedal, and capable of using tools. The story's setting was the English Lake District. Perhaps Jeremy Fisher was modeled after rumored sightings around Sunray Gardens near where the author grew up," explained Kareem.

"Authors tend to write about things they've seen. That… It's an interesting theory," said Carson.

"What I am hearing is they have found this mineral in England, and we have an author writing about a walking tool using frog. We have the mineral found in Indiana where a green amphibious creature attacked a woman. You mentioned Egypt, where Heqet was the goddess of fertility. Depictions show her as a frog, or a woman with the head of a frog. Now we have found the mineral here in Ohio and four-foot tall, seventy-five-pound bipedal frogs have been seen. That seems to be the connection. Everywhere the rock has been found, people see bipedal frog-like beings," said Ty.

"That sounds like there are a lot of similarities. If those accounts are accurate, these creatures have been here for hundreds of years. I still feel like we are thin on what these creatures are, even if we are making some connections. I wish we had more to go on. I'm still disappointed most of the files we brought back from Phoenix were thick, but the one for Loveland was smaller than I expected. Stuff we could have found with a quick internet search. If it were more complete, we could be prepared for what we're up against here," said Carson.

"I think the best thing we can do is head back out for another nighttime investigation."

CHAPTER 12

BIG RED MACHINE

Half-past ten and Carson and Ty were still asleep in their rooms. Although unseen by them, Kareem and Tegan were as well. A typical morning routine following a nighttime investigation. Somehow, Carson opened his eyes, at least mid-way, and forced a turn onto his back. Barely conscious, his left hand dropped onto the top of the end table and secure his cellphone. With a slow and wobbly hand, he forced the phone in front of his face, and once again closed his eyes. A deep breath and his eyes opened again, at least mid-way.

He saw the notification for a received text from the middle of the night. The text preview showed no name or number as the sender. Instead, it displayed anonymous. It was likely spam. Probably someone was trying to reach him about his auto warranty. But what if it wasn't? Hesitating for a few seconds, Carson tapped the message and read the text:

If you want to know about the Frogmen, meet me at 665 Service Rd in Loveland

Staring at the message, he caved in and replied to the message.

When?

Almost instantly, he received a reply.

Sunday 5 p.m.

Carson did not respond, but gazed at the screen running scenarios in his mind. Ty squirmed in his bed, rolling from side to side.

"Whatcha doin' up so early?" asked Ty, muffled under the comforter.

"Got a message asking to meet up on Sunday. They claim to have information about the Loveland Frog," Carson said.

The response caused Ty to sit up in his bed.

"Who is it from?" asked Ty.

"Dunno. Only says anonymous."

"Are you going? Are *we* going?"

"Don't see why not. We still need answers, and maybe this can help solve some mysteries we still have," Carson replied.

"Maybe it's a trap."

"From who? A rival cryptozoology gang? I don't see the harm in seeing if it's a legit lead or not. Even if we're wrong and it's nothing, we still get ice cream…" replied Carson.

"I scream, you scream…." Said Ty.

"We *all* scream for ice cream," answered Carson.

"I have a text too," stated Ty. "My dude Lemmy is going to pick up the trap and meet us at the new location tonight. He said he's going to make a few modifications to the trap.

"Good! I think we are in a good area, but maybe move down a little south," answered Carson.

"I'll text Tegan. Let's get some breakfast. I'm ready to eat!" said Ty.

Carson pulled over along the faded, cracked blacktop of County Road 255, and pulled over.

"This ought about to do it," said Carson. "I called Lemmy, and he's going to meet us here. I think we were close yesterday, but we got lucky. The small run leads to the river, but Emily said yesterday that the treenbergite was a key to the mystery. We don't know what these frogmen want with it, but the evidence must be more than coincidence. There is some connection between those minerals, the trees we saw scratched up, and these frogmen," he said.

"And that mineral is found along the river, so we should be a little closer to the source," said Ty.

"I think we can do it," said Carson. "Lemmy built a great trap. Unfortunately, we didn't get to use it. We caught a

glimpse yesterday, but we must prove the myth wrong or the myth right. And getting these things in that try is how we'll do it!"

"We have the thermal camera again tonight and we've got these head lamps. It was too hard chasing it and using the flashlight yesterday. Now we each can wear a headlamp to see what the hell we're doing and have a free hand to take on these creatures," replied Ty.

Light faded as the sun hung low in the sky. Headlights approached, signaling Lemmy was here.

"How ya'll doing tonight?" asked Lemmy.

"Doing good, but we'll be better if we get these guys in the trap tonight," replied Ty.

"I made a few modifications today, so hopefully it will help you. It's a little heavier, which I figured would help it be sturdy in case these guys had a fight in them, and the extra weight would cause the overhead cage to drop faster," Lemmy said. "I replaced the bamboo with some reused lumber from an old barn."

"Is that why it's a faded red?" asked Kareem.

"Yes, most of the paint has chipped off over the years from the weather. They tore this down about six months ago and it's been sitting in the sun, drying out. That caused the paint to curl, but she'll do the job," Lemmy replied.

"We'll help you get it placed. I figure we've got a good two hours before we get good darkness out here," said Carson.

"Hopefully that rain will hold off," said Lemmy.

"I hope so. It's already cold out here. We might see a bit of snow, but I don't know about the rain. We've got these head lamps, but that moon's giving off some descent light too," said Carson.

"The full moon is a day or two away, so it should give you good light out there," said Lemmy.

The weight of the trap was heavier than last night. It took two men on each side to carry each wall of the trap down the small trail to the base near the bank of the river. The downhill descent and increasing darkness made the journey more challenging than it should have been. A journey they would repeat six times before all components were at the desired location.

"Now to assemble it here, then we can set it with the dirt, mulch, and these rocks," said Lemmy.

"I don't know the utekite is going to do anything. After talking to that woman at the bar last night, I think we were wrong about that," admitted Carson.

"And we only have a couple pieces of treenbergite. Probably not enough to attract them," said Kareem.

"If those stones are found around the river, and the trees are an indicator of the stones, let's see if we can't find the trees around here. Maybe use that as bait," suggested Tegan.

"That's a good idea. Ty, you said the sap comes from scratched bark and trunks. Maybe these creatures have learned the scent from the resin can be a sign treenbergite is near," theorized Carson. "If it's the stones they're after, perhaps the scent of the trees will draw them toward the trap?"

"It must give off a powerful scent," said Ty. "one use the website stated was cosmetics."

Kareem, Tegan, and Carson spread out, searching for a Styrax tree while Ty and Lemmy put the last additions on the trap assembly. Kareem's headlamp reflected off a nearby tree.

"Hey guys, I think this is one," suggested Kareem.

Ty rejoined the group with his cellphone, opened the identification app and snapped a photo of the tree.

"Yes, got it. Let's take a few scrapes of the bark from this one and put inside the trap. That should draw them to it," Ty stated.

Carson removed a small pocketknife from his jeans and whittled off several small pieces of bark.

"Scatter these on top of the dirt and mulch inside the trap," Carson said, handing the bark to Kareem and Tegan.

Lemmy looked over the ground and up at the hanging lid of the trap. He walked around and put a hand around posts, giving them a little shake and pull.

"Pretty sturdy, which is what I was going for," said Lemmy. "These things aren't frogs, from what you say. It's easy to dismiss frogs as small and not focus on the strength of the trap, but if they are almost four feet tall and over seventy pounds, they can do some damage ramming that weight into the walls. This barn wood should give it enough weight and sturdiness to keep them contained until you guys can get back and see what they are," he said.

"We gotta make sure we do this right," replied Ty. "We need the trap to hold them, but first we've got to get these creatures to the trap. We're going to find them and drive them up this way."

"You're right," said Carson. "And I think we should start on the north side up here and on top of the hill. Take the high ground and push them down the trail to where we're set up here. I hope that the tree will attract them. Most animals have a heightened sense of smell and it's not unexpected to think these things have one too. Even if they are… something else," said Carson.

Later that evening, Lemmy was long gone, and the group searched the cold, dark woods looking for the Ohio Frogmen.

"Damn, it feels different tonight," said Tegan.

"It's a little colder than yesterday," responded Kareem.

"Not that. Like the energy. Makes your skin almost crawl," said Tegan.

"It's thick back here," replied Ty as the trail appeared to disappear in favor of thicker brush and undercover.

"Look for any signs or tracks," said Carson. "And keep your eyes open for scratch marks in these trees. That's a sign they're close. Don't let your guard down," he instructed.

The group stopped walking as a rustling sound was heard through the leaves.

"Shhh! Do you hear that?" asked Carson.

"Last night's frost helped crisp up these leaves," said Ty. "Gives us a good audible tracker."

"Yeah, I thought I heard something in the leaves over here," Carson said, turning and pointing down the bank leaving to the river.

"We're downhill now. Sound could be bouncing off these rocks and trees and making it sound over there when it's maybe closer to us," replied Kareem.

As they continued to follow the trail, they heard creaks and cracks that caused them to walk slowly and navigate at different speeds. Carson looked around and saw they were spreading apart.

"Hey, let's close it up a little tighter… Let's get a little tighter," he warned. "Don't get too far ahead… Easy now."

"You got that thermal, Tegan?" asked Ty.

"Yeah, right here," she said, scanning it from left to right along the trail.

"Keep that thermal working on both sides," instructed Carson.

Another loud rustle up the hill drew their attention.

""You get that? I heard him going through the leaves," said Kareem. "There!" he yelled, pointing to a shadow image up the hill. "Let's get him!" Kareem shouted as he took the hill, running into the darkness as Tegan attempted to get the creature on the thermal. "I got this one!" they heard fading as Kareem ran up the hill toward the source.

"Get the hell back here!" yelled Carson, realizing that while Kareem thought he was chasing one creature, there likely would be three. And three against one wasn't good odds.

"I can't see him. Is he out there?" asked Tegan excitedly.

"Damn it!" yelled Ty.

"Talk to me, Kareem!" shouted Carson.

The woods were quiet. The gang stared at each other and listened, hoping to hear something. A couple minutes later, they heard crunching gravel and crushed frosty leaves.

"I could see it, but barely got my light on it," said Kareem, out of breath.

Tegan continued to use the thermal, panning it to see if she could pick up the trail again.

"I can't get him on here," Tegan admitted.

"Let's move the way we want him to go," suggested Carson, bent over and wiping his brow.

"Now that you're okay, it surprised me how quick you could move up that hill," said Carson.

"I still workout," replied Kareem. "You guys alright?"

"You damn right I'm alright," answered Carson aggressively.

"Looks like we're back at the beginning," said Tegan.

"No, they are still out here, and so are we. Let's get these damn things," stated Carson.

Kareem and Tegan recognized Carson was getting tense. The constant feeling of him against the scientific community who wouldn't admit these hidden animals existed bubbled up and affected his decisions. They knew when that happened, he started making small mistakes. Mistakes that increased the risk to the team.

Ty also displayed that feeling occasionally, but not to the extent Carson did. Kareem thought made them fast friends back in college. However, now that they were older and maybe a little slower, it caused them to risk injury: shoulder bites from chupacabras, attacks from lake monsters, or cuts and scrapes from supernatural camels.

"Be alert," Kareem whispered to Tegan as they continued, not hearing anything for several minutes.

"Let's keep pushing down toward the trap and maybe we will jump them and get this night over with," Tegan stated.

Carson and Ty caught up with Kareem and Tegan and stood in a closer formation. Each member focused in a different direction, waiting for one of his or her senses to trigger. He hoped for either audible or visual clues. Tegan especially did not want to encounter a sensory or tactile experience.

The trail led them closer to the edge of the river. They stopped at looked at the river. It was mostly dark even with the moon's light reflected off the surface.

"Keep your eyes peeled," said Carson. "They might be attracted to running water. Maybe he went down here. We've got to be ready for anything," he said.

Moments later, he lost his balance, tripping over something on the riverbank. It was a dark brown bottle sunken in the mud from the recent rains, sticking up high enough to be a nuisance to passersby. Carson looked down at the culprit, his headlamp shining on the label. It was an empty dark brown barrel bottle reading *Wiedemann Bohemian Special Fine Beer.*

"Wiedemann? Damn. My old man used to drink that," he said, staring at the label for several seconds before moving on.

"One thing I always remember on these night hunts, everything changes. This is not our world. If we go out, we might not be the hunter. Animals have the upper hand in the dark. Their eyes are better adjusted, their hearing and olfactory senses are more equipment, and they are familiar with the terrain. All areas where we have the disadvantage," said Kareem.

"The forest changes depending on who steps foot on it," said Carson. "Maybe if we take this little foot trail that goes up the hill here, it will loop back down to the river up a head. If we can get around them, we can drive them back up toward the trap," said Carson.

"At least catch one of them," stated Ty.

The noise in the woods picked up as the researchers heard more tree branches crack and break. The leaves played an increased symphony of footsteps.

"I'm hearing things out there," said Carson. "Talk to me guys!"

"It's all around," stated Kareem.

Tegan frantically panned the area with the thermal. A tree branch cracked loudly, drawing Tegan's attention.

"Right here beside us, she shouted as another branch cracked.

"Where? I don't see shit," said Carson.

"Look out guys, he's right here," she said once again.

"I see one of them, over there, let's go," Kareem said, again excited to see something.

This time, the rest of the group kept up with him. They could only make out a brief flash of grayish-green skin as the bouncing light of the headlamp occasionally hit the back of the running creature. They could tell there were three individuals, but each was fast. Much faster than the human pursuers could keep up with. The gap between hunter and hunted increased, ultimately the hunted showed its prowess by escaping danger.

"Damn!" said Carson, pulling up and attempting to catch his brief.

"At least they are headed in the right direction," stated Ty.

"Yeah, we can only hope…."

Bang!

The group stopped hearing the loud sound of the trap lid slamming down on the four balls below it.

The group stopped and looked at each other in disbelief.

"Holy…! That's the trap!" Carson yelled.

All four turned and ran toward the hill, Kareem again leading the way. Tegan, Ty, and Carson arrived, standing about four feet from the triggered trap.

"Look, there's something moving in there," said Tegan, pointing to the downed roof of the trap.

"What do we do now?" asked Kareem. "We don't have any weapons."

"We don't need a weapon. We got them. Looks like three in there," he said, walking closer toward the trap to see if he could get a better look. The rest of the group took individual steps toward the trap.

As Carson got within two feet of the trap, one of the captured frogmen returned his stare. A brief encounter that likely seemed much longer to Carson. The creature raised his left hand. He was holding something, but Carson couldn't tell what it was. Then a quick, bright blue spark flashed, causing each of the group to react by throwing up a bent elbow to shield their eyes from the light. Each instinctively dropped to the ground. Opening their eyes didn't help as each bat of their eyes repeated the temporary flash blindness caused by the creature's tool, blocking and washing out their central and peripheral vision.

After a few minutes, Carson was the first to crawl.

"Damn, what the hell was that?" he asked.

"That must be the wand," Ty said, still with head on the ground, his hands pushing down on the road, still hunched over on his knees.

Kareem and Tegan stood up with a wobbly effort. Tegan flashed her eyes to work through the exposure.

"Guys," she said, pausing. "They're gone, she said nervously, shining her head lamp into the cage.

"I'll be damned!" Kareem said.

"Where the hell did they go? The trap's down," Carson said frantically, standing to his feet and running circles around the wooden structure, searching for any sign of damage. "This thing's solid," he said. "No way could they break out!"

Ty jumped up as well and joined his friend in exploring the perimeter of the cage.

"I don't understand," Carson said, stupefied.

"Must be that wand," stated Tegan. "When I heard the other stories, I thought the wand emitted light that blinded people...," she stated.

"It does," added Kareem.

"Yes, but I thought it then allowed them to run away and escape. There was no escaping the trap. They must have teleported," she stated.

"Teleport," Carson repeated, looking around and letting it soak into his mind.

The three guys looked at each other, then Tegan, then the fallen tap in disbelief. Even with finding the frogmen and chasing them toward the trap, the team hadn't gotten a good look at them to see what they were and now that they had been transported away from danger, they wouldn't get that chance now.

"Everything was going right for us there. Now these!" Carson said, still stunned.

Ty stood bent over, hands on knees, pondering the possibilities.

"You said the other day they were aliens," Ty said to Kareem.

Kareem nodded his head without a word.

"There are a lot of questions to be answered," said Carson. "Beginning with what these are, where they are from, and what do they want here."

"Now I'm more eager than hell to get these things," said Ty.

"I think we need to come back and do one more nighttime investigation. This time down the river at Chateau Laroche," said Carson.

"Let's get back to the hotel. There's nothing more to do here tonight," said Ty. "And besides, I picked up some beers earlier that I was hoping we would be opening tonight in the room to celebrate, but I see that's not going to happen."

They started up the hill and back to their car before Ty stopped.

"Hey Carson, be sure you open the trail camera on the side of that tree and get the card," Ty said.

"Trail camera?" asked Carson.

"Yeah, when Lemmy and I put up the walls of the trap, he added a camera there to see if we could capture any images of the beings," Ty said. "We can put the card in my laptop back in the room and see if we got anything."

"What beer did you get? Speaking of getting something," Kareem replied.

"I got a twelve pack of a variety of beers from around town," he said. "I found a carry out not too far away and picked up a handful of local stuff."

"That's nice!" said Tegan.

"It was drive-thru also," replied Ty.

"Let's go back to the hotel, enjoy the beers, and look at the SDS card," said Carson. "It's been a hell of a night… Hell of a night!"

CHAPTER 13

FROG WENT A-COURTIN'

Ty was the first to wake up. The sound of housekeeping running the sweeper in the hallway interrupted what was a deep, restful sleep. He rubbed his eyes with one hand and dragged the hand across his face, trying to reclaim his senses. He tuned his head to the side and saw Carson fall victim to the vacuum's loud noise.

"Jesus, why so early?" Carson mumbled somewhat audibly.

Ty placed his hands on his chest and pulled one high enough to read through squinted eyesight.

"Dude, it's almost eleven. Time to get up anyway," replied a still tired Ty.

Trying to raise up, he noticed they both were still in the clothes from last night. He took a deep breath and theorized it exhausted them chasing the creatures in the woods. There was a huge high from catching the frogmen in the trap, but then a rapid crash after the team realized they had escaped. The impact of that adrenalin crash coupled with the late night of after full, long day likely caused them to fall asleep, dead to the world. To all, except the mighty vacuum cleaner of the Motel 6.

Carson dropped one foot to the side of the bed and reach the standing position first. He staggered to the bedroom wall and braced himself up. He dove a hand into his jeans pocket and removed a receipt, the other room key, and the SDS card from the trail camera last night.

"Damn, bro. I forgot about this shit," he said, holding it up for Ty to see.

"Oh, snap. We should call Kareem and Tegan over to check it out. I'll get the laptop fired up," Ty stated. He reached for the phone first and sent a text next door to Kareem, then clicked the on button on his Toshiba.

"Plus, we got beer for breakfast," Carson called out from the other room.

"In all fairness, it is almost lunchtime," Ty validated. "I still can't believe we trapped those things yesterday, and they got away."

"Yeah, it was a great night until then," Carson replied.

"How would we have known? We barely know anything about these creatures. Only bits and pieces," replied Ty.

"For now," Carson replied, looking at his phone. "Maybe after we meet this tip tonight, we will have something," Carson stated.

"I wouldn't get too excited," said Ty. "It's probably some troll. Did you give someone your number?"

"Not that I recall," replied Carson.

"There you go."

"You're right. At least we have this SDS card to remove when Kareem and Tegan come over. That's something," suggested Carson.

Later, Kareem and Tegan sat on one bed in Carson and Ty's hotel room. While Ty loaded the card into the laptop, Carson tended to the beers in the refrigerator.

"Who wants one? Random pull," asked Carson.

Three hands went up as Carson turned and reached blindly into the fridge and pulled out a cold can. He tossed one to each of his friends. Kareem caught a Sonder You Betcha!, Tegan a Braxton Garage Door, Ty a Braxton Tropic Flare, and Carson pulled a Fretboard Vlad.

"We have enough for one more each," announced Carson. "You ready, Ty?"

"I'm getting the files pulled up here," he said, sitting on the floor with Tegan and Kareem, looking over his shoulder. Carson joined Ty down on the floor, leaning up against the nightstand. "Let's see what we captured," said Ty.

As the folder icon appeared on the screen of Ty's laptop, he double clicked it to reveal nine photos the camera captured.

He started at the top and double clicked the file to open the image. The first image captured the trap, but nothing else.

"Something must have triggered it, but I see nothing in the frame," Carson said, staring at the image.

Ty opened two more images, only seeing a blurry image in each. "Could be a bug? There's something there, but it looks small and blurry."

The fourth, fifth, and six photos revealed something. One individual that was unlike anything they had seen before. With the night vision photo, the darkness was a dark green, while the image of the creature was a lighter washed white green.

"Damn, I think we got one," said Carson. "Hard to tell what color it is. With the shading of night vision it could be green, gray, white… we don't know for sure, but it looks like that's our creature," he said.

"Look further behind it. There's something else behind it," said Kareem.

"That's another one of them," said Tegan. "I think that's its hand right there," she said, pointing to the corner of the image.

"Reports have stated there are three beings. This one looks like it's operating the point, while the other two fall back," suggested Ty.

The creature in the front appeared to be over three feet tall and a little chunky for its height. However, the face was too blurry to get a good look. As the crew continued to view the photos, the next few proved to be clearer.

"Look, this one is clearer. It's looking almost right at the camera!" said Carson.

"Right here I think they knew we captured them on camera," said Ty. "They backed away to leave but walked into the trap. Look, in this next photo, one has a small shovel and is digging!" he said.

"Probably trying to get that treenbergite," suggested Tegan.

"He dug and activated the trap mechanism," said Kareem. "Look, the next picture shows the roof collapsing on the top of the trap," he said pointing to an image of three beings inside the trap looking up and the roof represented by a blurred image showing its motion downward. One creature appeared to be wearing a small bag or pouch around its waist.

"Oh wow, here's their escape!" Ty said as the next image showed one creature holding the wand. The photo showed a solid white area illuminating from the wand, meaning it generated a bright source of light. The eighth image showed the trap empty, the shutter likely triggered by the fleeing creatures.

"You can almost see one of their legs still in this photo as the light expands and fills the entire image," said Tegan.

The last image was an empty, dark trap.

"Damn, did you see those things? Those last images were pretty good, don't ya think?" said Carson.

"I can see how people think they look like frogmen. They are smaller than a person, a little round, and their facial features have a round head that resembles a frog," said Kareem.

"But with small ears, and almost gill like fins behind them," said Tegan.

"Their head looks wrinkly, and their eyes have no pupils," replied Carson.

"It resembles the *Creature from the Black Lagoon* a little," added Ty. "Maybe there is a connection to the Indiana woman that saw something like the movie.

"I know they haven't attacked many people, but it looks like they have some sharp teeth," replied Tegan. "Hopefully they are only for show!"

"They seem to be timid," replied Kareem. "Every time we have been near them, they run away, and there aren't many witnesses who were attacked."

"Few, but Vivian was chased. The woman in Indiana was grabbed, and who knows how many unreported stories there are. I am sure even today in these parts of the country that are small town and rural, they don't talk about strange happenings too often. People might talk about them and make it difficult to live in the area without ridicule," replied Tegan.

"They appear to be the size of a child, and I see the similarity to frogs, but unlike amphibians that we are used to seeing, these are still active in the cold weather. They appear to be nocturnal, based on most of the sightings, unless it is cloudy," Carson said.

"I think we have to go with Kareem's earlier statement about them being alien. As you said, their behavior does not match what we see with other amphibians, and they are bipedal. However, for me, the deciding factor is that wand. They held it up, a bright light emitted, and they were out of the trap. We thought before it temporarily blinds the victim, allowing time for escape, but this trap was down. They couldn't have escaped through the sides. It must be something supernatural, or perhaps extraterrestrial," said Ty.

"Aliens again," replied Kareem.

"In Phoenix we saw aliens, but we didn't encounter any," replied Carson.

"Tegan, how are you feeling? If that's accurate, at least they aren't frogs," stated Ty.

"But they look like frogs, and that's creepy enough," Tegan replied. "I'll need that second beer."

Carson stood up and pulled the last beers from the fridge.

"Here's one that will make you feel better. It's a fruit beer," he said, handing Tegan a Sonder Kings Island Blue Ice Cream Ale. To Kareem, he handed a Streetside Suh, Brah? IPA and Ty a Schwarzbier. The last beer, a bottle of Mayan Sacrifice from Darkness Brewing, he kept for himself.

"I will get back with Lemmy on the trap. It held up pretty well against those creatures, but that wand was something that couldn't be accounted for," suggested Ty.

"Our research and eyewitness reports told of a wand object that emitted light, but we didn't know what that meant. I thought it was an escape mechanism to buy some time. If that were the case, the cage would have still held them," said Carson.

"Hopefully we learn more this evening with your hot tip," suggested Kareem.

"Let's hope so," said Carson.

That evening, Carson parked the car along Service Road and the group began walking toward the address he wrote.

"665 appears to be an old-fashioned ice cream shop," Carson said. "Looks like it's the place," said Carson, standing at the front door.

The others walked in the held-open door and looked around for a seat. The restaurant was empty. A couple of people were sitting at the counter, two people sat at a round table in the corner, and one old man was sitting alone at a large table that appeared to seat six. A server was in the back running the sweeper across the rug in the back of the large open room.

"Maybe that's our guy?" asked Ty, looking at the old man.

Carson led the way to the large wooden table with a decoupage tabletop.

"Excuse me, sir. I'm Carson Quinn and I am wondering if you are the person who texted me the other day?"

The old man was sitting at the table with a bag of Wendy's fries and a large chocolate shake with the lid removed. He dragged a fry through the top of the shake as Carson introduced himself.

"Matter of fact, I am," said the old man. "Please, sit and I will tell you everything you need to know about the Loveland Frog."

Ty and Carson looked at each other with anticipation and took a seat across from the old man. Tegan joined them and Kareem sat next to the informant.

"Name's James Fritz," the old man stated.

"Nice to meet you, James. How are you?" replied Carson. "How do you know about the Loveland Frog? We are eager to learn more about them."

"I'm holding true. Since you said *them*, I take it you've seen them? You know it's more than one," asked James.

"Yes, we were on their trail a few nights ago, but yesterday we saw them, at least running away. Luckily, we had a trail camera set up and captured some images," Ty said.

He pulled out his cell phone and opened some images he transferred.

"Yep, that's them," said James, looking at the phone.

"We heard many people talking about these things, but we couldn't catch up with them. I thought maybe it was like the Tulpa Effect, where people were visualizing and manifesting these things, but those photos on the trail camera changed that. Things were going well, and we caught them in our trap, but when we closed in, they disappeared. Almost seems like they teleported out of there," said Carson.

"They did," said James.

The investigators glanced at each other in disbelief but also comforted by the revelation they were not crazy.

"How do you fit into this puzzle?" asked Tegan.

"As I mentioned, my name is James Fritz. You might think what I am about to tell you is a crazy, highly unusual story," he said.

"That's just our game," added Ty.

"I am a former police chief here in the city of Loveland," James said. "And my father also was the police chief."

"There were some historical eyewitness reports we found in our research," said Carson. "Did you see anything in your time as Chief?"

"One of those reports you may have read about was Officer Ray Shockey, Jr.," replied James. "As he approached in his vehicle, the creatures scattered. Two ran off, but one stood up and looked at him for a moment before it climbed over the guardrail and went down to the river," remembered James.

"Yes, we read the accounts of his experience," replied Carson.

"I was his Chief," replied James. "It was 1972 and Ray said he observed multiple creatures having a conversation on the side of the road.

"What was your impression when you heard his report?" asked Tegan.

"I was a little surprised and checked it out myself with one of my other officers," said James. "Ray was visibly shaken from the experience, but it only intensified afterward. He was a rookie cop in a small, highly religious community. After word got out, fellow officers ridiculed him, and the community wondered if he was trustworthy. They look to police for stability and security, but a cop who reports a three-foot bipedal frog gives many a cause for alarm," he said.

"How did Ray handle the repercussions?" asked Kareem.

"He held true to the story despite ridicule," said James. "We went to the scene of the incident, and we found scratches and abrasions on the guardrail where Ray said the creature went over the bank," reported James.

"He must have felt relieved that you could back up his story," added Tegan.

"We didn't see the creature, but I talked to Ray about the incident and tried to get him to stop and change the story, but he didn't. We had an officer's own sighting, but we had to mute it. Police testimonies in court hold high regard. I didn't want to jeopardize his credibility. But despite my requests, he didn't change his story," said James.

"That was 1972? There was another incident around that time also, wasn't there?" asked Carson.

"Yes, Officer Mark Matthews, a few weeks later," replied James. "He was one of the officers who once ridiculed Shockey, but then saw it himself a few weeks later."

"Two incidents. Seems like your guys were on to something," said Ty.

"When Matthews reported his sighting, the ridicule continued from other offices and the community outrage increased again," said James. "The Commissioner called me and told me to step in and handle it. I told Matthews we couldn't have this because it was causing outrage and fear in the community. We can't have the community living in fear. I forced him to recant his story and say it was a large, escaped iguana. In small rural areas, stuff like this is not talked about," he added.

"Did that do the trick?" asked Carson.

"Yes, for the most part. Once he came out and said not only was it an iguana, but he shot and killed it, the community returned to normal and the fear faded," said James.

"But you knew that wasn't accurate?" asked Tegan.

"Yes, I knew. I joined the Loveland Police Department in 1970 at the age of twenty-four. Prior to that, I was an MP in the Army, serving from age eighteen in 1963 until I was discharged in 1969. Once I got out, I worked for a year on the force and began Chief at age twenty-five. I was twenty-seven in 1972 when these stories happened," James stated.

"Twenty-five and the Chief of Police? That's pretty young," said Ty.

"It is, but I had the benefit of my dad being a former Police Chief for the city as well," James said. "Being young, even with my father having been Chief, I didn't need those stories disrupting the town and impacting the city's perception of me being able to lead. It worked, but I still had Shockey. Pressuring Matthews to recant showed the strength of Shockey's story because he didn't cave in."

"Did you believe Shockey?" asked Tegan.

"Yes, I knew what they were from my time in the Army," stated James. "Well, let me back up a bit," he said, dipping another fry into his shake. "My father was John Fritz, who was Chief back in the 1950s. If you did your research, you know the first sighting of these frogmen was back in 1955 with a young man named Robert Hunnicutt. He was a prominent businessperson who was a non-drinker and churchgoer in the area. He told my father he was traveling about 4 a.m. and saw strange little men about three feet tall under a bridge," added James.

"That would be a surprising sight at that time of day," said Ty.

"His first impression was that somebody was hurt, or some crazy guys were having fun," replied James. "He was curious, and in case it was someone needing help, he stopped his car and got out for a better look. To his surprise, he discovered the figures were non-human and about three feet tall."

"Did he get a good look at these non-human creatures?" asked Kareem.

"He stressed that the creatures were not green, but a greyish color. He said they were wearing garments. These tight-fitting clothes stretched over a lop-sided chest that bulged from the shoulder to the armpit. He reported one arm looked normal proportion for their body, but the other was much slender, noticeably longer than its opposite member. He got a fleeting impression of something baggy, but weeds and brush obscured the legs. He said their heads were ugly, reminding him of a *frog's face because of the mouth which spanned, in a thin line, across a smooth grey face.* He thought the eyes, although without brows, seemed normal, but yellow without pupils. He also mentioned the nose was indistinct. The top of the head had a painted-on-like-hair effect, like a plastic doll. He described it as corrugated or like rolls of fat running horizontally over a bald head," James reported.

"And there were three of them? That's what we saw too," replied Carson.

"According to Hunnicutt, the middle biped, and the one closest to him, was first seen, with his arms raised a foot or so above the head. He said it was holding a dark chain or stick, which emitted blue/white sparks jumping from one hand to the other. As he approached the creatures, he said this biped then lowered its arms and made a slight unnatural move toward him, as if motioning him not to come any closer. He stated he stood still, watching for about three minutes, too amazed to be afraid. Next thing he remembered, he was on his way to dad's office. After he reported the encounter, my dad stationed an armed guard there in case it was men up to no good. Dad said that the incident was investigated by the FBI," revealed James.

"The FBI?" asked Ty.

"Yes, dad called his findings in to the government, and they told him to say they found nothing. The government investigated the incident over the next few years and concluded in the 1960s regarding the creatures' origins," James said.

"That's an incredible story!" said Carson. "But why are you telling us now?"

"I'm an old man and have cancer now. It's terminal and I know I have little time left. People still don't talk about the unknown too much around here, even though strange things happen. It's still taboo and people don't like to talk or share their stories. Now I'm near my deathbed and want to set the record straight. With my time short, I focus my current life path on truth," he admitted.

"I'm sorry to hear that," said Tegan. "There is still a lot of stigma regarding these types of encounters, but we are hoping through our work to change that. With cellphones in every hand and people's increased connection to the internet, these stories are increasing. People have always seen things, but now they are telling about their experiences more often as they have the tools to film and get the word out there."

"I was in the bar the other day with Cora. I was sitting there wearing my Bengals gear. I overheard you talking about the frogmen and after you left, I asked Cora for your card. Carson dropped it and Cora picked it up, placing it near the register. I decided then to reach out to you. This was one wrong I wanted to right before I pass," revealed James. "Cancer lets you see things from a new perspective. Let's you see how things are, which is why I want to set the record straight."

"And you think the creatures your dad saw in 1955 are the same ones you investigated in 1972?" asked Ty.

"I know they are, and the same ones you saw the other night," James said, dipping another fry into the shake. "Let me clarify. Same species, but different individuals. I know what the creatures are, what they want, and everything about them. They have been here for a long time and likely will continue coming back until their mission has concluded."

"Mission? What mission?" asked Carson.

"Time to show you how the sausage is made," replied James. "Sharing this I might get my comeuppance, but I have little time, so it doesn't matter."

"After what we saw on the trail camera yesterday, and how we captured them in our trap, but they escaped, we speculated they were extraterrestrials. When we first sat down, we said it was as if they teleported out of there. You said they did. What can you tell us about that?" asked Ty.

"During my time in the Army, they stationed me in multiple places. Indiana, Cambridgeshire in England, and at a secret base in Phoenix," said James.

"Phoenix? We were there, and we found an underground base hidden beneath a dam," said Tegan. "We found an alien spaceship, tools, and several files."

"Dreamy Draw. Yes, that's the place," replied James.

"We found and removed many folders, and most of them appear to be thick with information, but there was a file on Loveland that only had a few pages included," replied Kareem.

"That folder is what led us here. We saw a video on YouTube about an encounter with these creatures and we remembered Loveland being one file we removed from that underground base," said Carson.

"But it was weird that it was so small compared to the others," Kareem added. "Why didn't we find this information in the Phoenix files?"

James reached into his jacket and removed a worn folder filled with aged papers that was from the Phoenix files. He said some files were removed back in the 1980s.

"I had been out of the army for over ten years, but still had connections to the base. Over the last eight years, since the reports from Shockey and Matthews, word had gotten out and Loveland was seeing more tourists looking for these frogs. I was afraid if the files were discovered, news would increase, and tourists would overrun the town. When the base shut down, they evacuated in a hurry. I made a call to a friend and asked him to pull the file before they left. I didn't care about the other files, only the one that affected me and my town. My friend pulled the files, but only got a portion," he said.

"The Loveland file we got from Phoenix seemed to be the main overview and didn't contain any details that we couldn't find online. I guess your friend got the bulk of the file," replied Carson.

"These are what you're missing," he said, handing the folder over to Carson.

Carson opened the folder and flipped through the large stack of papers describing Loveland Frogman incidents of 1955, 1960, 1972, and 1974, including reports and analysis from Project Blue Book investigations.

"Project Bluebook? If the government knew what these beings were based on these case files, why would they keep it a secret? There haven't been many attacks, but these creatures have been seen several times," asked Tegan.

"Mainly to prevent the spread of fear and what would happen if people questioned what we know about our world and our religions. Religion is a big money business, especially today. If people heard aliens existed and were visiting Earth, it would not only cause fear spreading, but it would also cause some things to not align with our societal beliefs. Go back throughout history. We can see ancient paintings from Egypt and other civilizations around the world possibly depicting spaceships. Earlier humans may have been more in touch with aliens than we are today," James said.

"Because of government suppression?" asked Carson.

"If they can control information, they control the narrative," stated James. "You mention the internet and getting the stories out there, but it is also easy to use it to influence the public opinion and steer them away from stories you don't want out there."

"You mentioned some places they stationed you, such as Indiana and England. We have heard people have seen these creatures in both places," replied Ty.

"Yes, they are attributed to Loveland because that's the first sighting that drew attention, but over the years, we have seen them elsewhere. The Bluebook reports have them even back in ancient Egypt near the Nile," stated James.

"Those locations you mention also relate to deposits found of a mineral called treenbergite that we recently learned about," stated Kareem.

"That is what they are on Earth searching for," replied James. "To them, treenbergite is a critical element to their species' survival and they must harvest as much as possible. The smell of Benzoin in the sap of Styrax trees attracts them. The resin causes them to go berserk with anticipation. They can use tools such as pickaxes or shovels. They find treenbergite in the ground, harvest it, and transport it back to their planet," said James.

"What do they want with this mineral?" asked Carson.

"These creatures are an alien species called *Xeephin Crireks* or *Xeephines*. They come from the planet Criri 46U in the Zeta Orion galaxy. It's a rocky desert world lit by two blinding white suns. Xeephines burn in sunlight and therefore they have searched the universe for solutions. They live in a vast network of gypsum caverns beneath the surface of their home world. This is not their natural habitat, but they were forced to move underground after a series of natural catastrophes," James reported.

"What are these Xeephines like on their planet?" asked Tegan.

"They do fight among other warring factions, but they only pose a mild threat to humans. They try to avoid them and use a light-generating wand made from Labradorite to teleport, allowing them to escape. They eat small mammals, but there have been isolated reports of attacks on humans if they are cornered," James continued.

"I am familiar with Labradorite from an occult shop I visited in Phoenix," stated Tegan.

"Labradorite is said to be the stone of magic," replied James. "It has been known by Inuits native to Paul's Island in Labrador, Canada for millennia, and more recently found by Moravian missionaries in the late 18th century. The stone is believed to have magical properties, and there are some extraordinary legends that surround its origin. In fact, some ancient Inuit legends claim that the rocks along Canada's northeast shoreline contained the Northern Lights. An Inuit warrior put a spear through the rocks to release the light, but wasn't entirely successful. It is, therefore, a thought that the iridescent colors within the rocks represent the light that remained trapped. Others believe the stone is frozen fire, which may be because of the brilliant copper and red tones that appear in the streaks of iridescence found in the stone," James stated.

"And this wand, we've seen the powerful light it generates. That's how they escaped our trap," said Carson.

"Yes, the magic in the wand allows them to teleport out of harm's way," James replied.

"What's their purpose here with finding this mineral?" asked Ty.

"The entire planet is under one planetary rule by a fair royal family. They have special soldiers known only as Guardians - the most powerful people in their world. They dispatched individuals specializing in science to other star systems to search planets for treenbergite. Older members of their species grow big bushy beards, but the Guardians sent to other planets are younger individuals. On their home, they live in small herds called pods and are nomadic. They have amazing eyesight, and the color of their eyes change with their mood. They can see the entire electromagnetic spectrum and they have a heightened sense of smell that allows them to locate the benzoin resin. They have three genders, and it takes all three to create an offspring. They can only survive on planets in a binary-star system. That's why they can't stay long on earth. They come here to search for the treenbergite, but then must return home. The leaders dispatch another group of Guardians to continue the search while the prior group returns home," James revealed. "They always travel in threes, one who uses the wand, one who is the harvester, and the one with a bag is the collector."

"The only sign we found of them was scratched bark from the Styrax trees, a couple pieces of what turned out to be treenbergite, a piece of selenite and some unakite," replied Kareem.

"The selenite comes from the Gypsum, which is akin to their home gypsum and limestone caverns. Unakite is found as pebbles and cobbles from glacial drift in the beach rock on the shores of Lake Superior, and they use it and other shiny stones for currency. Off-world minerals such as unakite are valuable in their society," reported James.

"But what do they use treenbergite for on their world?" asked Carson.

"The richest members of society go on a pilgrimage to a waterfall in the mountains whenever there is an eclipse because of the dangers of being in direct sun," replied James. "The crystal structure of treenbergite is unique and a one-of-a-kind mineral in its class, mostly because of its rare hexagonal crystallization. They used it in solar geoengineering to partially block the sun's rays. Their society believes that by finding this mineral and geoengineering it on their planet, they can create a protective shield against the rays of their suns and allow them to return from the underground caverns to the surface of their planet," said James.

"What should we do with them?" asked Kareem.

"I would let them be," replied James. "They pose little of a threat to humans. They search for treenbergite at night and return home when they have collected a large amount. They are spotted occasionally, which causes shock for the witnesses, but they are not typically any danger. It may cause them individually to question their beliefs and worldview, but as long as we minimize it and prevent it from going to a widespread global phenomenon, we should be fine with the status quo," said James.

"I still think we should search for them again. Maybe we can learn more about them and our universe," suggested Carson.

"We haven't been successful in communicating with them, but they are a communicative group among individuals. We haven't been able to translate their language," stated James. "I recommend not attempting to trap them. They are here to go about their mission and save their planet. They don't need to be harassed and captured," he suggested.

"You've been a big help," said Carson. "I would like to go out again, but not to capture them. Only to make contact and understand. I dedicate my life to searching for unknown animals around the world and understanding the mysteries of life. Imagine the mysteries that are in the universe. I want to believe and to understand more."

"Good luck with your investigation. Stay safe out there," James said as the group walked out together with him.

After the door closed, a man at the bar reached down and texted from his cell.

Commander Williams, the team has been in contact with James Fritz, sent Field Agent Garfield Blanchard.

Moments later, a response stated, *End of Watch for Chief Fritz*

Carson found parking at the Fireman's memorial off Harrison Street, and the team walked the short distance to Narrow Path Brewery. The brewery, located a stone's throw away from the banks of the Little Miami River, offered an excellent selection of beer and a spot to reflect and plan the final nighttime investigation.

"This has been another wild trip," said Kareem.

"How fortunate that we met James. It's interesting how often minor events that seem insignificant can lead to larger outcomes. I didn't realize I dropped my card at the bar, and he was there and witnessed it. What are the chances that the former Chief of police in Loveland, a man who not only investigated the 1972 sightings, but whose dad was Chief of police in 1955 and worked the original investigation happened to be in the same bar?" asked Carson. "And his connections to the Army, to the Phoenix secret base, and Project Blue Book connected the dots."

"It's fortunate these Xeephines aren't here for anything more than saving their planet," said Ty. "Imagine having to travel thirteen thousand light years to another planet to retrieve materials capable of saving your home? Those Guardians are not only intelligent, but brave in taking on that mission."

Following the primitive dirt trail from the back parking lot to the brewery, they passed a large yard with a lighted walkway and multiple tent-covered tables.

"It's cool, but not too chilly tonight. Do you guys want to sit outside at one of these tables?" asked Tegan.

"Better than the Texas heat," said Carson.

"I'll go inside and grab a couple of menus," replied Kareem, as the rest of the group secured a table.

As Kareem returned to the group, server Chris Davidson accompanied him.

"Hello, everyone. Glad you could join us tonight. I brought some water to start you off while you look at the menu. We have some specials in the brewhouse this evening," Chris stated.

Carson, looking at the menu, took notice of a bottle called What Lies Beneath. The image on the menu showed the image of a man appearing to struggle from drowning in a river and an animal lurking in the background.

"That looks like it could be an alligator, but being from Loveland, maybe it's a giant frog," mentioned Carson. "How much is the bottle, Chris?"

"That's gonna set you back nine dollars."

"Sold."

"I will bring it and a glass for you. Anyone else know what they want?" Chris asked.

"That one sums up our adventures in Ohio," said Kareem. "Trail Chaser works too."

"Partially Redacted," ordered Tegan.

"Drinking Gourd for me," said Ty.

"Tomorrow we should conduct a final nighttime investigation to get a better look at these beings and see if we might understand them a little more. The thrill of interacting with an alien species is something I have dreamed about since I was a kid, and who would have thought we would have that opportunity here in Cincinnati?" said Carson.

"Those sci-fi shows always interested me when I was younger, added Ty. "We're here. They're here. I say we do it."

"We found the spaceship in Phoenix, and that opened my eyes to what I thought was only fantasy," replied Tegan. "But one thing I understand, since we have been conducting these investigations into mysterious creatures, is the path between myth and reality may be narrower than you think."

"I've always felt it was unlikely we were alone in the universe," said Kareem. "How many stars and planets are out there? It is crazy to think in a continuously expanding universe where stars are born and die that we are the only beings in the universe. It shocked me when we found what we did in Phoenix, but now, it's exciting and I'm ready to see them first-hand. Imagine what they could teach us?"

"Okay, that's settled. Tomorrow night let's head to Chateau Laroche for our last investigation and see if we can connect with the Xeephines," said Carson.

CHAPTER 14

HOT DAMN! IT'S THE LOVELAND

FROG

"C'mon, we have to get going," shouted Carson from the hotel parking lot as Kareem headed back toward the room instead of getting in the vehicle. It was getting late in the evening and the temperature was dropping. Despite the cold, the forecast called for thunderstorms with heavy rain. The crew still brought headlamps to wear while investigating the trails around Chateau Laroche, but the full moon would aid them again.

Despite using this investigation as a happy connection with an alien species, Kareem's dreams the night before adumbrated a feeling that things might not go according to plan.

"I have to get something from the room first," he yelled to the group waiting below.

Inside the room, he opened his suitcase, pushed the clothes around, and retrieved the object he sought. He placed it in the inner pocket of his jacket and scampered down the stairs to the waiting car below. "Sorry. Ready now," he said once inside.

"Finally," said Tegan.

Carson sniffed the air. "What's up Tegan? Ready to hit the club after this hunt?"

Tegan and Kareem looked at each other in the back seat. She was dressed for hiking in the nighttime woods and wearing a waterproof insulated coat in case it rained, but she had applied a few sprays of perfume.

"I felt that this is not only our final nighttime investigation, and it feels good to be wrapping up another mystery, but this is our first opportunity to meet an alien species. I wanted to make a good impression," Tegan said.

"This should be a different investigation. In the past we hunted to capture the creature and identify what we are up against, but this time we already know what it is and there isn't much reason for concern," said Carson.

"This should be a good location to find them. Many of our eyewitnesses were close to the castle and over the past couple of nights, we have found them in the area," said Ty.

"I think the castle is the magnet. The apex of the activity. Right here is where it all goes down," said Carson.

They parked along the road in front of the castle. Night fell and the full moon rose. It was time for them to enter the forest at night in anticipation of a friendly encounter with an alien species.

"This is where the paranormal team shot the video that set us off on this journey," replied Ty. "Let's get the equipment. Let's do it!"

"Let's get a selfie of the group with the castle in the background," suggested Kareem. "Maybe we will get lucky and can get a selfie with the alien visitors later in the evening," he said optimistically.

As they stepped foot out of the vehicle and took a few steps toward the trail, the gravel ground and the grass crunched from another early frost. They set off down a narrow dirt path that edged the riverbank, disappearing into the wooded darkness. Without the need to search for evidence slowing down their progress, the group continued deeper into the woods, hoping to encounter once again the trio of visitors.

"It's crazy being so deep in the woods, how all the sounds and facets of modern life faded away," said Tegan.

"Being in the forest, you can't help but wonder what happens in the thicket of the woods. The parts where you can't walk. What's off in these woods where there is no path?" said Kareem.

"I don't know," said Carson. "Whenever I'm deep in the forest, I feel connected to nature. It's almost as if you tap into the Mother Nature energy of it all when you're lost in the trees."

"All I know is tonight feels like it's more difficult than I expected. This is a long ass hike, uphill the entire way," complained Ty, struggling with his breathing. "I thought I was in better shape than this!"

"Heading in the gates back there when we were starting out and getting our stuff, I was excited and ready to rock and roll. Now, the feeling has changed out here. It's damn creepy," replied Carson.

"I think it's this weather. The full moon was providing good light, but I feel the storm rolling in and the energy is different. It's a little unsettling and now it's dark out," replied Ty.

"We're in the forest, and I can't see," replied Kareem. "These headlamps don't seem to work."

"It's dark and I'm getting an uneasy vibe too," said Tegan.

"I think I see a clearing over there. Down the winding forest path," said Carson.

"I literally can't see shit," replied Ty.

"I think Carson's right. Looks like a narrow path over there. The full moon gives it an ominous feeling. Those dark clouds rolled in front of the moon, darkening the woods even further," added Kareem.

"I dislike this feeling. It's like being in a horror movie right now," replied Tegan.

"It's your imagination. Remember, we have nothing to worry about here. Don't let the night shadows play tricks on you," added Carson.

"I heard a noise. You all hear that?" asked Ty.

"Yes," said Tegan and Kareem.

"What the hell is that?" asked Carson. He called out into the night, "Hello?" However, there was no response. The group heard a creaking noise and spun around to search for the culprit.

"That's freaky right there," said Carson. "I know I heard something."

"Feels like there are footsteps behind us," Ty said.

They continued deeper into the dark woods, searching for signs of the Xeephines but were unsuccessful.

"Tonight is about the damn freakiest night we could have picked to come out to the forest because it is raining now, there's a full moon, and it's pitch-black aside from these clouds. Like zero light," said Kareem.

An unexplainable, odd noise off in the distance caused everyone to stop in his or her tracks and listen to the woods.

"That was bizarre. Really strange," said Carson.

"We all heard it," answered Tegan. "Honestly, this is probably one of the scariest places I've been to in a long time!"

"Is there anybody here in the forest?" Carson again called out after hearing a noise. He listened, but heard no response. "We've been walking down the path for about forty minutes now. We're deep in. I would have thought we would have found them by now," he said. The only response was cricket and other bugs noises, but even those quieted as they continued deeper into the woods.

"God, I do not like this. I can't believe we're doing this right now. You owe me some beers on this one," Tegan replied.

"C'mon, this was supposed to be a fun investigation. We know they are not scary monsters, but intelligent beings trying to save their world," said Carson.

"Yeah, maybe on paper, but this is fucking terrifying, serious *Blair Witch Project* vibes," replied Ty.

"I'm hearing creaks and growls out there, man," said Kareem.

A crack of thunder rolled, and the rain intensified.

"Damn, it's starting to freaking pour!" said Carson.

"I hate investigating in the rain," replied Kareem.

"Is there anyone in the woods?" shouted Carson. He waited, but again received no response. "Can you use your voice and tell me if you're here?" Again, no response.

"I don't think it's the visitors. I think there is something else out here in these woods," said Ty.

"Bigfoot?" asked Tegan.

"I don't think that's it," answered Ty.

They came upon a random pathway that led deeper into the woods.

"Let's go this way," suggested Carson. "I feel compelled to follow it. Seeing as my intuition usually leads me to interesting discoveries, maybe we should split up," he suggested.

"Are you crazy? It's already scary as hell here," said Kareem.

"But we have found nothing. Let's try it for a minute to see if we can locate them. You have your radio?"

"Yeah, we have one," replied Tegan.

"Ty and I will head down the path alone and you two work the main trail. I think ours curves around and rejoins the main path up ahead," Carson said.

Ty and Carson took the obscure path to the right while Kareem and Tegan continued ahead. A few minutes later, Carson and Ty were in a different world.

"Walking down here, only the two of us… and holy shit, is it terrifying," observed Ty.

"It got icy cold right here," Carson said, running his hands in a circle around him.

Lightning flashed overhead.

"I doubt many people have taken this path before, because it is terrifying!" replied Ty.

Carson listened intently.

"This takes a lot of guts. I'm so freaked out, but I'm trying to keep my cool."

"We don't normally get this worked up. We've been doing these investigations for a while now, but something feels off here," said Ty.

Kareem and Tegan continued following the main path, searching for signs of the beings.

"Something's weird right here. There's something sinister about these woods," said Kareem.

"You don't have to tell me," said Tegan. "I feel it too."

"Is there anyone here in the forest with us?" called out Kareem, but as Carson experienced, there was no response.

"Without Carson and Ty, these woods are not cool. I feel the air is getting heavier, and it feels like some awful shit is about to go down," said Tegan, scanning the areas for any signs of friendly life. "This cloud cover and rain is not helping,"

Kareem began singing *Cold November Rain* to lighten the mood. Tegan reported it was not working.

"Something's damn noisy and it sounds like it's following us. Keeps coming from the woods," said Kareem.

"Murder victims? Spirits of Natives?" asked Tegan.

"Shit wouldn't surprise me either way right now," Kareem replied.

Ty and Carson continued down their path. Carson saw what appeared to be something stone through the trees. Walking down the path, it darkened further. The storm clouds removed the full moon, and the duo only had the flashlight on their heads to light the way.

"Dude, what the fuck is this?" asked Carson as they came upon the remnants of an old homestead. The only thing remaining was the burned down section of an old chimney.

"Old-ass chimney in the clearing. Just being here is dark and intense. I feel like we literally need to run out here. Who knows what happened there? I'm getting some bad vibes from this entire area. Literally consuming. I have a black feeling. There's a lot to deal with energy wise," said Ty.

"I keep feeling like we're being followed. I'm overcome with an extreme sense of dread and anxiety, as if something bad is about to happen," replied Carson. "I think we need to meet back up with Tegan and Kareem, pronto!"

Ty and Carson stopped and looked around, unable to gain their bearings.

"Walking through the forest, really deep in here, I can't even see the path we came on. Look for another point of entry," replied Carson. "It's like I'm disoriented.

"This is scary, man," said Ty. "We're in the damn thick of it here!"

"That's enough for me," said Carson. "I think if we stay on this path a little longer, we will meet back up with the others."

The sound of gravel crunched under their feet with each step, although dampened by the leaf-cover. Soon, they found a break in the trees, and it put them back on the main path. Carson called out to Kareem.

"Hey, where are you guys?" he shouted. "He awaited a response, and soon he received it. Ty and Kareem began jogging up the trail to catch up with Tegan and Kareem.

"You guys okay?" asked Kareem.

"Yeah. This place does not disappoint. It's scary at night, and I don't scare easily," said Ty.

"Any idea where we are?" asked Tegan.

"Not a clue. I think we are north of the castle, and we've been out here a while, so maybe a couple of miles? But I'm not getting any cell service in these trees," Carson said.

"Damn, I remembered something," said Kareem.

"What's that?" asked Ty.

"Remember Buck and Parker talking about the ghosts at the Castle?" asked Kareem.

"Yeah, the old man who built the castle?" replied Ty.

"Yes, but there were other ghosts. One was a woman who died from a moonshine explosion. In a cave? Out here in these woods? What if it's her?" asked Kareem.

"The White Lady," spoke Tegan.

"We should try to calm down. These Xeephines have an excellent sense of smell. I don't want them smelling our fear," stated Ty. "Shit might go down differently if that were the case."

The path began a slow climb before turning right at the top of a small hill and continuing to ascend.

"Damn. This is too much," said Ty.

"What is?" asked Carson.

"All of it – the hill, the rain, the cold, the clouds, this dark-ass vibe in the woods. I'm like, damn, what else could go wrong?" replied Ty.

"Do you hear that?" asked Kareem, scanning the area, searching for the source of a rustling noise he thought he heard in the leaves?

Tegan stumbled through the thick forest. She looked at the fallen foliage and the aging, rotted bark on the large trees that surrounded her and wondered how she ended up in such a place. The weather was chilly, nipping at Tegan's body, despite the coat she wore. She alternated between holding herself close and running her free hand over her body to spread warmth, but it did little to ease her discomfort. Soon, the group reached a small clearing where the forest's canopy opened, allowing the moonlight, once again escaping the dark clouds, to peek through.

Suddenly, they heard a rustle from behind. Tegan spun around and gazed at the shrubbery, but found nothing.

"What was that?" asked Ty.

"I don't know! I'm picking up noises all around me!" added Kareem.

Soon Ty would have the answer to his question. They paused, seeing two Xeephines ahead communicating with themselves, while one was digging. The cool autumn breeze picked up, causing the visitors to stop and take notice of the scent of the nighttime intruders.

"Jesus, there they are!" said Kareem. "But I'm still hearing something scamper through the surrounding leaves, but I see nothing."

Tegan watched and took a couple of steps when she heard another rustle, followed by a dull thud. Before she could turn around to look, there was another thud, but this one was because of something smacking into her at the midpoint of her back. She turned to see one of the visitors behind her. She discovered that something was an enormous tongue from the creature's mouth. It loud out a guttural growl and its sharp teeth gleamed in the moonlight. The tongue was coated with a strange thick wetness that became sticky, catching her coat and preventing her escape. The guys turned to face the sound of what was the third Xeephin approaching from behind. The visitor's attack terrified Tegan, but she unbuttoned and slipped out of her coat. The disturbance drew the attention of the other two creatures. Each sniffed the air, causing their eyes to grow bright yellow. Soon, they joined in the pursuit.

"What the fuck?" yelled Carson. "I thought these things were supposed to be shy and afraid of humans?"

Escaping from her coat and darting into the darkness, she turned around to face her assailant, and was terrified at what she saw. The Xeephin wasn't the small, timid creature that they had seen on the trail camera images, but it appeared to be larger and transformed with a long pink tongue retracting into its mouth with jagged teeth. Its wide maw smacked and slurped in anticipation of its target.

Tegan ran, overcome with fear and disbelief at the events. She saw the creature seemed to focus on her more than the others and decided her survival was more important than standing around and watching. She ran as fast as she could in the opposite direction of the team. Even as she continued, the creature wasn't far behind. As it closed the gap, the creature's tongue smacked again into her back. She cried out in fear as it yanked her backwards towards the frog's open mouth, now expanded much larger than previously observed. Clawing at the ground, she tried to get a grip on something to free herself, but the soil was too soft, and the leaves were loose. The stickiness of the creature's tongue held fast, and she could not stop the pull toward the creature. She felt that this was the end, then something unexpected happened. She felt the impact from what appeared to be a wave of purple light. The strike left her entire body tingling and her vision blinded.

It wasn't long before the tongue pulled her toward the frog's mouth. She could not fight off her assailant. Its lips closed rapidly, rubbing against her. With another pull of the tongue, it drew her into the frog's open mouth. She screamed in terror at her predicament, but the frog ignored it and continued its consumption. She struggled, attempting to break free, but was unsuccessful. The visitor continued, pulling her in ever further. Its jaw tightened to hold her in place. As she could not pull herself out, Tegan tried one last time to get some leverage. She lifted her feet, forcing herself to lean back deeper into the frog's mouth. Her feet sat on the edge of its dripping maw, and she pushed down with every ounce of strength she had. Unfortunately, her plan backfired, and her feet slipped off the creature's lips and into the frog's waiting mouth. The last of her hope taken from her and completely trapped, she could only cry as the frog's tongue detached from her back and slathered saliva all over her. With one final slurp, Tegan's head joined the rest of her body in the mouth, its flesh covering her on all sides. She disappeared inside the creature.

"Nooo!" screamed Kareem. Ty and Carson stared in disbelief. Instinctively, Kareem pulled an object from the back of his jeans and fired it at the visitor. Ty and Carson charged the other two visitors, which turned and ran. A ray from the weapon Kareem unleashed hit the cannibalistic frog in its chest, causing it to scream in a painful outburst before disintegrating instantly.

As the creature exploded, Tegan's body fell to the ground, released from the visitor's stomach. Kareem tucked the weapon back into his waistband and ran toward his friend, who lay lifeless on the cold ground. Grabbing her by the shoulders and shaking, she moved and groaned, feeling a mix of pain and shock. He lifted her head up and comforted her. The slime from the alien's mouth still covered her.

Ty and Carson continued to pursue the other two creatures.

"Let's keep the heat on them!" shouted Carson.

"I've got the angle on him," Ty said as he lunged toward the second frogman, capturing it by its feet and knocking it to the ground.

Carson continued after the third frogman. He glanced over to see Ty wrestling the second one on the ground. Carson ran at the other visitor, then dove at him in an attempted spear. The frogman stopped, raised his slender left hand, revealing the wand. A blue light burst from the device, blinding the two men, forcing Ty to bury his face in his elbow on the ground. Carson's leap ended in an empty flop on the hard, cold ground. Immediately he buried his eyes, heavily watering from the blinding light, into his elbow on the cold ground. When the men opened their eyes, the blue light faded, and Ty was on the ground alone. Carson was also on the ground facing where the third frogman had been. Both creatures were gone.

"Fuckin' A! What happened?" Carson shouted, confused. He walked over and helped Ty stand up. They looked around and saw Kareem tending to Tegan, who was lying on the ground where the exploded frogman had been. They jogged over to her and joined Kareem in comforting her.

With backup present, Kareem stepped back into the clearing and called 911 from his cell. While on the phone, he nervously looked around, still feeling an unseen presence around him. He was on edge after the attack on Tegan, and every noise increased his anxiety, even though he couldn't see anything. It sounded like scampering feet through the leaves, but the remaining Xeephines were gone.

The medics got Kareem's location from the GPS on his phone. They instructed someone to remain with her until they arrived, which Kareem volunteered to do. Ty and Carson walked down the hill and stood at Catalpa Road, where it bends into Shore Drive. It took about fifteen minutes for the EMS to arrive. Two medics removed a gurney from the back of the ambulance and headed up the hill, following Ty and Carson to Tegan's location.

Once on the scene, the medics found her responsive and Kareem sobbing uncontrollably while holding her hand. One technician began asking pertinent medical questions centering on past medical history, current medications, allergies, physician's name, and hospital choice, while the other began the examination and treatment. They placed a mask over her face to receive oxygen while the second technician administered an IV for fluid administration.

She drifted in and out of consciousness as the ambulance crew placed her on the stretcher and descended the hill. Once safely at the bottom, they placed her into the ambulance where they began transport to Bethesda North Hospital. Kareem ordered an Uber to take them back to their vehicle at the castle. The trio remained in silence on the way to their car and later, the ride to the hospital.

It was ninety minutes before the guys could see Tegan in the hospital. When they were granted entry, she was laying in the hospital bed, hooked up to instruments to monitor her vitals. She was asleep.

"We gave her something to make her comfortable and allow her to rest," said Dr. Willie Borland.

"How's she doing, Doc?" asked Kareem. "She's like my sister."

"The next twenty-four hours may still pose some risk, but I think she'll be fine. She needs to rest. We'll hold her overnight for observations, but you should be able to pick her up tomorrow, assuming there are no setbacks," he said. "What happened to her out there?"

The men looked at each other and their thoughts raced, trying to figure out what to say.

"She fell," said Carson.

"It was dark up there and we didn't see there was a little pond that had frozen over," added Ty.

"The ice broke, and she fell in. We got her out, but not before she was under for several minutes," said Kareem.

"Hmm, well, she doesn't have hypothermia. Some minor injuries and shock. She'll be okay. Whatever happened, good thing you boys were around when it did. Otherwise, she wouldn't be here. You should go home and get some rest. I'm sure it was a stressful night for everyone," he said as he exited the door.

Sitting in the hospital parking lot, the guys thought about the night's events.

"The breweries are all closed now. Want to hit up a dive bar in the area?" asked Carson. "Might not be hurt to get something to eat, and I could certainly use a drink to take the edge off."

Kareem and Ty nodded in agreement. Cindy's Friendly Tavern was seven miles away and close to the hotel, and it was open until 2:30 a.m.

"Nothing we can do for her tonight, I guess," said Ty. "That was some scary shit. I didn't know those creatures would turn like that. What the hell was up with their eyes and mouth? Those jaws expanded and transformed into something like *Alien*."

"It was something alien," added Kareem. "I don't know what worked them up. They had been afraid of humans in most of the eyewitness accounts."

"They went right after her. As soon as they saw we were there, one pounced behind and attacked. Fucking swallowed her whole," relived Carson.

"But we've been close to them two other times and nothing like that happened. What was different tonight?" asked Ty.

"Remember, she was wearing perfume tonight?" asked Kareem. "I wonder if that was it? What was it?"

"Hey, you're right, she was. We'll have to ask her about that tomorrow," replied Carson.

"And speaking of *what was it*, what the hell did you use on that alien?" asked Ty.

"That was the weapon I pulled from the spaceship in Phoenix," replied Kareem.

"Weapon? You've had it all along?" asked Carson.

"Yes. That's what I went back into the hotel room to get this morning. I know we were saying this was going to be a fun investigation, and we were going to contact this alien species, but when I woke up this morning, I had a bad feeling. Like my dreams last night foreshadowed what was going to happen, so after I started down to the car I went back and got it from my suitcase," Kareem said.

"How did you get it through security at the airport?" asked Carson.

"It's not metal, and I learned how to tear it down and reassemble it," Kareem said. "It was in pieces in my suitcase and parts hid in the zipped lining with my cologne and toiletries."

"I'm glad you thought ahead to bring it. You saved her life back there," replied Carson.

CHAPTER 15

MEMENTO MORI

Just before eleven, the guys were at the hospital to pick up Tegan. They walked to her room while she had a final checkup with Dr. Borland. It was still less than an hour after visiting hours began and the hospital hallways were still quiet. The team passed only one young man before reaching Tegan's room. After passing the exam, she was discharged. A nurse arrived to load her into a wheelchair. Carson jogged back outside and moved the car closer to the hospital entrance as the nurse pushed her through the discharge doors.

A young candy-striper at the information desk pointed to direct the young man from the hallway to a side waiting room, where he stopped to make a phone call.

"Field Agent Garfield Blanchard for Commander Williams," he waited while the receptionist attempted unsuccessfully to reach the young man's commanding officer.

"Let him know there's been an incident with the Xeephines," stated Field Agent Blanchard.

"How are you feeling?" Carson asked.

"Still a little sore, but physically I think I'm okay," Tegan replied in a still weakened voice.

"How about otherwise?" asked Kareem.

"That… that might take some time," she replied. "A lot of shit ran through my mind last night while in the hospital, and still this morning. I mean, I was still dealing with some hesitation and uncertainty since we left Phoenix."

"I don't know if you're up to talking about last night, but we were talking after we left the hospital. Those creatures reacted differently than they did the other two nights. I remember you were wearing perfume. What was it?" asked Carson.

"It was Bijou Romantique. Something I wear frequently when I go out. It's my go to perfume," she said.

"Do you know the ingredients?" asked Ty.

"No, not really. Why?" she asked.

"Just curious," replied Ty.

"I have my cell phone here," she said, leaning to the side to retrieve the phone under her leg. "The website says, *Top notes are Ylang-Ylang, pink pepper, bergamot and lemon; middle notes* are iris, Clary Sage and coconut; base notes are benzoin, vanilla and vetiver," she read.

"Benzoin? That's the same thing that is in the sap from those trees that get the Xeephines worked up," said Ty. "They smell it and think there is treenbergite in the area, and because that is important to their survival, they go apeshit."

"Damn, you're right. I remember James telling us about that. I didn't think about it when I put it on yesterday," Tegan said.

"The only instances where they attacked were you yesterday and Vivian when she was out there," said Kareem. "I wonder what perfume she wears?"

"I have her number. Let me check with her," replied Tegan.

Hey, just curious, what perfume were you wearing the other day? Because you smelled amazing, she texted to Vivian.

Moments later, she received a reply. *Kurkdjian's Cologne pour le soir.*

She copied the reply and searched the internet for its description. She found the answer, *Infusion of benzoin from Siam [aka Siam Resin], cumin, Ylang-ylang, Bulgarian and Iranian rose honey, incense absolute, Atlas cedarwood, and sandalwood.*

"That must be the connection," she said. "Both perfumes contained benzoin.

"Are you up for getting out and walking around?" asked Carson. "We have some time before our flight back to Austin this evening."

"Yeah, some fresh air will do me good. I hate being in hospitals. So stuffy and sterile," Tegan stated.

Downtown Loveland, on the south side of Main Street, east of the intersection with North Elm Street and Loveland Madeira Road, sat a small shop next to a deli by the Loveland Artist building. Inside, it was filled with mummified creatures, mortician tools, freak show relics, and other curiosities. It was called Memento Mori: Shop of Weirdness.

"This is a nice stop on our way home," said Kareem. "I love these oddities. Check out that brown bear wearing a saddle. That's one guy I wouldn't like to ride."

"What does *Memento Mori* mean?" asked Carson.

"It's Latin for *Remember you will die*," replied Tegan. "Seems pretty fitting."

"That was a crazy encounter last night, but at least you didn't die," replied Kareem.

"I'm not so sure. Physically, I am here, but… there are parts I can't remember and… I don't know. I feel somehow different now," replied Tegan. "I had a legit near-death experience. The doctor said that he has studied near-death experiences for decades and much of what he's learned has been hard to square with prevailing notions of how the mind and brain work," she said. "We think the mind and the brain are the same. They're inseparable. However, that might not be the case. He has conducted research on persons with heavily disabled or even measurably inactive brains, and he says his evidence suggests a near-death experience can cause the mind and brain to dissociate under extreme circumstances. The mind can continue to function when the brain seems to stop," she said.

"What did you feel yesterday?" asked Kareem.

"The Doc said what I was feeling was common. I had vivid hallucinations and out-of-body sensations. I sensed floating above my body in the hospital bed, and I could recall events that took place during periods of apparent unconsciousness," she said.

"When were you unconscious?" asked Kareem.

"For a time, I was unconscious when the creature swallowed me, then in and out during the ambulance ride, but it was a rough night in the hospital too. I don't think it lasted long, but I suffered a minor setback, and the nurses came running to attend to me," she revealed. "To be honest, the doctor told me I died on the way to the hospital, but they revived me. I was aware of being near death. I had a surge of pleasant, almost euphoric sensations. Time slowed down. I had encounters with god-like entities, and even deceased loved ones. I also had a lucid recall of memories. Almost like a detailed highlight reel of one's life. You know how they say right before death your life flashes before your eyes? I thought for a moment during the night that I would not make it. But they helped me pull through," she said.

"Damn, I had no idea. That's some heavy shit," said Ty.

They walked around the shop looking at the interesting items, but left without making a purchase. Carson checked his watch.

"Time for one more stop before we head back to the rental car return?"

"Fine with me," replied Ty.

"Let's hit up Arnold's Bar & Grill. It's Cincinnati's oldest continuously operated food and drink establishment, dating back to 1861," said Carson.

"What do you think happened to the Xeephines?" asked Tegan.

"I am positive that the one that swallowed you is no longer with us," said Kareem. "The other two? Who knows? They used the wand to transport out of there, but did they go home? Probably not. I expect they will return to complete the mission of finding treenbergite to save their planet."

"Are you hungry? I hear they have a small food menu, but it's good," replied Carson.

"No, I don't think I can eat right now," said Tegan.

"I don't blame you. I'm good too," added Kareem.

"I will probably get something light to drink," replied Carson.

They took a spot on the large patio and awaited the server. A young woman with short red hair approached to take their order.

"A Little Kings for me," replied Carson.

"B.O.R.I.S. The Crusher," said Ty.

"A Bürger Classic for me," said Kareem.

"The Razz Treaty," replied Tegan.

"Coming right up," replied the server. "Any food I can get you?"

"No, we're good right now, thanks," answered Carson.

Waiting for their drinks, the group enjoyed the unseasonably mild and sunny afternoon. Tegan frequently stared off into the distance, watching cars and people pass by, and being silent. When she spoke, the guys were surprised.

"So… I was thinking," she started. "You guys should go back to Austin without me."

"What? What do you mean without you?" asked Carson.

"The last twenty-four hours have been difficult, and I need some time. Some time to process everything and I don't know, reflect on my life, and my choices," she said.

The server returned with their drink order. She brought an empty glass and the bottle of B.O.R.I.S. for Ty. Looking down at his choice, he was a little taken aback.

"Damn, that was insensitive," he said, looking at the bottle with a label containing a large frog.

"It's cool. I'm feeling okay with my phobia," said Tegan. "I don't feel it as strong now."

"Getting back to your news bomb, Jourdyn already booked our tickets for this evening," said Kareem.

"I called early this morning before you guys arrived, and I changed my ticket."

"When did you change it for?" asked Kareem.

"Right now it's open. I don't know when I will come back, but I will. Don't worry," she said.

"Where will you stay?" asked Carson.

"I know a guy here. Actually, his name is Guy. Guy Buffalo. He's a friend and a therapist," Tegan said.

"Guy Buffalo? That's actually his name?" asked Kareem.

"No, his name is Guy Kelley, but in college, he played on the football team as a fullback and was known for running people over, so they nicknamed him Buffalo. It stuck, and we called him Guy Buffalo," she said. "He's a psychiatrist I met back in school, and I reached out right before I changed my flight. He has a house with a little casita I can stay at for a while."

"I don't know what to say," said Carson.

"No, it's okay. This is good," Tegan replied. "I need some time to sort things out and research this near-death experience activity. Maybe it goes away, but I feel different today and what was normal seems out of line," she replied.

"For certain, what we do is not normal," replied Ty. "It is niche. It's unusual, and often it is scary. Search for unknown creatures and you never know what you'll come up against. I don't get scared easily and I enjoy this stuff, ever since I was a teenager, but I admit yesterday, I was scared. The vibes felt dark and off all night. I couldn't shake it, so I understand. I felt similar feelings after being bitten by the chupacabra down in San Antonio. It took me a while to feel right again," Ty admitted. "You take all the time you need. We'll be waiting when you're ready."

Carson stood and looked at his watch.

"I'm speechless. Are you sure? You're staying here? If that's what you want…don't stay away too long… We have to go if we're going to return the car and make our flight."

"Yes, I'm good. See ya around, Carson," she said standing up to hug him.

She gave Ty a hug that she held for an extended period, then finally Kareem.

"You keep your phone on. I'll be talking to you," she said.

Tearfully, Kareem embraced her and asked again if she was certain.

"I don't know what I will do without you always around harassing me," he said. "We're like siblings at this point."

"You'll be fine," she said. "See you soon," she said, blowing him a kiss as the guys turned to head back to the car.

EPILOGUE

Inside the space proclaimed as *Cincinnati's First Brew Lounge*, Tegan sat on a black, no leather sofa placed against the wall. She looked out the window with a sense of nervousness and relief. Her friends headed back to Austin, and she was awaiting another friend, a local therapist she knew as Guy Buffalo.

She hadn't seen him since college, but back then, they were wonderful friends who talked deep into the night about life and philosophies. After the events of the last day, she felt that was what she needed most. Carson, Ty, and Kareem were great to talk to. They were like family, but this was different. She needed to talk to someone with a similar professional background to her.

Guy arrived, wearing dark jeans, a gray classic-fit crewneck sweater with a white undershirt, and a pair of black boots. He looked relaxed, yet professional, even for the weekend. His short, graying, stylish hair with matching trimmed beard and mustache exuded an aura of trust and comfort. Despite the years, she felt like she could talk to him, and he would listen, professional and unbiased. She and Kareem were close, but many times, he geared his advice toward what she *wanted* to hear, and not always what she *needed* to hear. Guy wouldn't have that consideration because they hadn't communicated in years.

"Hello, Tegan. It was great to get your text. How are you?" Guy asked, walking in and taking a seat on the no-back leather sofa across from her.

"Well, Guy, I've been better. I don't even know what to think anymore. Can I get you a beer?" she asked.

"No thanks, I don't drink," he replied.

"Do you mind?" she started

"No, not at all."

She motioned for the server and ordered a Karma double IPA.

"Seems appropriate after the last couple of days," she said.

When the beer arrived, she didn't know what to say or how to begin. She confessed confusion in her life, including her work as a therapist and her experiences hunting cryptids. She held the glass to her mouth, ready to sip from it, when she paused and chuckled into the beer.

"I don't know what to say here. I'm the therapist. People come to me for advice. It's hard to ask someone else for help when I am the one used to giving it," she admitted.

She recalled saying something similar earlier to Kareem. She recognized her experience in the woods heightened these feelings, but they existed before the trip to Ohio.

She told him about experience with death. He told her about his work with patients who were dealing with similar experiences, and how the event changes you. Sometimes subtly. Sometimes drastically. Things that seemed routine may no longer fit into this new life. As she expected, Guy was a good listener and easy to talk with about sensitive topics.

They discussed how the event altered her and what she was feeling now. She was sometimes shy, uncertain about going on investigations for unknown creatures, but certainly fearful of frogs. She discovered after being eaten by a large intergalactic frog, she no longer felt that fear.

She told Guy she was not afraid of death. She knew now that death was not the end. During her experience, she still felt alive, but differently. She realized space and time didn't exist in the way she assumed. During her travels in what felt like the afterlife, Tegan felt like she was gone from the human world for many years. In her mind, it was as if she had been away for a long time, but to the team, it was only a few minutes.

After moving through what seemed like a white light, Tegan found herself surrounded by six higher beings, all dressed in black. She felt comforted and loved by these beings and knew they were there to help her, but they seemed to stand there. She instinctively knew that they were communicating telepathically, but she had to learn how to quiet her mind to hear them. Once she learned how to keep her mind still, she could hear the beings ask her if she wanted to continue or go back to earth.

She told Guy that after she died, she underwent a life review where she got to experience all the lives that she had lived to date. Tegan said they made her watch, and even live through, multiple past lives including her present life. The experience was so real, it was as if she had to live through each one of her lives day by day. In that moment, she knew what lessons she came to earth to learn. If she didn't go back to her current life, she would still have to face these lessons at some other point.

One of the biggest takeaways from Tegan's experience was that she understood all beings are connected. She described how we are all stardust. This isn't some strange concept, she reinforced. We are all made of stardust, so we comprise the same matter as the sun, the stars, and the surrounding galaxies. All the beauty and power seen in the Universe also lives within us and is us.

"In your profession, and in your personal life, you are there for others. To help them, to guide them. That is your life calling. You are an empath and feel what others feel. Your purpose may be to help those who cannot progress and grow on their own until you step in and show the way. You are not a shy, uncertain girl. You are a leader who is capable of great things. You are no longer afraid of death and what it might bring because you have seen the other side and came back. Nothing can stand in your way or harm you now," Guy said.

"I feel a change in my level of fear, as if it is no longer there," she said.

"Experiencers often show a marked change in their attitude, not only toward their own life, but toward the lives of others as well. They are more open, caring, and loving, which you already were. Now you may be more so. However, some may also reexamine their existing relationships, ending some that are now not compatible with their new beliefs and attitudes. This seemingly new person often confuses the experiencer and family members, and problems can arise. Families can have a difficult time adjusting to the new normal," Guy said. "Another common side effect is that experiencers can become highly intuitive and often report an increase in perceived psychic experiences, including telepathy. You were taught how to communicate in this manner by the beings you encountered in the light. Use these gifts to explore your new life and persona. The old Tegan perhaps did die in that alien's mouth, but a new Tegan lives on. Maybe it's time for your own adventure and to explore this new reality," he concluded.

Like old times, they talked into the night, until the bar closed. Heading home, she was eager for a new day and to see what the future would bri

BEER LIST

16 Lots Brewing Company Razz Treaty Wheat Beer

Austin Beerworks Sputnik Imperial Stout

Big Ash Brewing Company Backbeat Coffee Blonde Ale

Big Ash Brewing Company Vanilla Cream Ale

Braxton Brewing Company Garage Door American Light Lager

Braxton Brewing Company Tropic Flare IPA

Cartridge Brewing Company Hollow Point Hibiscus Ale

Cartridge Brewing Company Opening Salvo Imperial IPA

Cartridge Brewing Company Sabot IPA

Cartridge Brewing Company Smokestack Smoked Beer

Christian Moerlein Brewing Barbarossa Lager - Munich Dunkel

Darkness Brewing Mayan Sacrifice Imperial Stout

Dead Low Brewing Schwarzbier

Esoteric Brewing Company Karma Double IPA

Fifty West Brewing Company Doom Pedal Witbier

Fifty West Brewing Company Punch you in the eyePA Imperial IPA

Fretboard Brewing Company Vlad German Pilsner George Wiedemann Brewing Company Wiedemann Bohemian Special

Fine Beer. Pilsner – Czech

Helio Basin Brewing Co. Chupacabra Logga German Pilsner

Highgrain Brewing Company Isar Weiss Bavarian Hefeweizen

Hofbräuhaus München Hofbräu Dunkel Lager - Munich Dunkel

Hoppin' Frog Brewery B.O.R.I.S. The Crusher Russian Imperial
Stout

Hopsquad Brewing Company Architetto Ruffini Italian Pilsner

Hudepohl-Schoenling Brewing Co. Bürger Classic American Lager

Hudepohl-Schoenling Brewing Co. Little Kings Cream Ale

Hudepohl-Schoenling Brewing Company Hudy Delight American
  Light Lager

Independence Brewing Company Power & Light Session IPA

Independence Brewing Company Stash IPA

Listermann Brewing Company Apricot Lemonade Parade Float
  Wild Ale

Listermann Brewing Company Bananas In Paradise New England
IPA

Listermann Brewing Company Cincinnatus Imperial Stout

Listermann Brewing Company Don't Talk Sh!t About Norwood
  Pale Ale

Listermann Brewing Company I'm On A Boat New England IPA

Listermann Brewing Company I've Had It With These
Motherf*****g
  IPAs At This Motherf*****g Brewery New England IPA

Listermann Brewing Company MannBeaverWolf Double Pastry
IPA

Listermann Brewing Company Prehistoric Bowl Crusher
  Berliner Weisse

Listermann Brewing Company Stylistic Abomination By Gummies
Double New England IPA

Listermann Brewing Company Team Fiona New England IPA

Listermann Brewing Company Yoda Potato Strikes Back
    Double New England IPA

Little Miami Brewing Company Peace Frog IPA

Little Miami Brewing Company Pterodactyl Hefeweizen

Little Miami Brewing Company Statesman Belgian Strong Golden
Ale

Little Miami Brewing Company Wang Dang Doodle Sour - Fruited
    Berliner Weisse

MadTree Brewing Odin's Breath Imperial Double IPA

MadTree Brewing Phantom Forest Imperial Double IPA

MadTree Brewing PsycHOPathy IPA

MadTree Brewing Thundersnow Scottish Ale

Miller Brewing Company Miller Lite Light Pilsner

Mt. Carmel Brewing Company Hibiscus Blueberry Blonde Ale Fruit
and Field Beer

Narrow Path Brewing Company Drinking Gourd Double IPA

Narrow Path Brewing Company Partially Redacted Wheat Beer

Narrow Path Brewing Company Trail Chaser Blonde Ale

Narrow Path Brewing Company What Lies Beneath English Brown
Ale

Nine Giant Brewing Bourbon Barrel Heavy Metal Drummer
    Russian Imperial Stout

Nine Giant Brewing Electrify Pale Ale - New Zealand

Nine Giant Brewing Hazy Mike D. Pale Ale – American

Nine Giant Brewing I Like Beeer! Blonde Ale

Nine Giant Brewing Interstellar Drift New England IPA

Nine Giant Brewing Murklord New England IPA

Nine Giant Brewing Save Ferris Berliner Weisse

Nine Giant Brewing West End Girls Porter

Rhinegeist Brewery Barrel Aged Penguin Imperial Stout

Rhinegeist Brewery Hustle Rye Pale Ale

Rhinegeist Brewery Peach Dodo Gose

Rhinegeist Brewery Red Wine Barrel Aged Night Whale Imperial
Stout

Rhinegeist Brewery Saber Tooth Tiger Imperial IPA

Rhinegeist Brewery Truth American IPA

Rivertown Brewery & Barrel House Roebling Vanilla Espresso
    Imperial Porter

Sonder Brewing Kings Island Blue Ice Cream Ale Fruit beer

Sonder Brewing You Betcha! New England IPA

Streetside Suh, Bruh? New England IPA

Taft's Ale House Cherrywood Amber

Taft's Ale House Cold Boy Pale Lager

Taft's Ale House Gavel Banger American IPA

Taft's Ale House Hazy Cabana Juice American IPA

Taft's Ale House Nellie's Lemon Frosty Ale American Pale Wheat

The Shop Beer Company Jackalope Pilsner

Thirsty Planet Brewing Company Thirsty Goat Amber

Urban Artifact Astrolabe Grape Ale

Urban Artifact Gas Light Double IPA

Urban Artifact Paperweight Fruit Beer

Urban Artifact Spyglass Sour - Fruited Berliner Weisse

Wren House Brewing Company Dreamy Draw Double IPA

Wren House Brewing Company Mercury Mine Triple IPA

ABOUT THE AUTHOR

Mark Trollinger is a fan of cryptozoology and craft beer. He grew up in Yellow Springs, Ohio and attended the University of Rio Grande in Rio Grande, Ohio - not far from Point Pleasant, WV, thus igniting Mark's interest in cryptozoology, beginning with Mothman. In 2012, Mark first tried Stone Brewing's Russian Imperial Stout, thus igniting Mark's interest in craft beer.

He is the author of *The Chupacabra and the Bat Rastard*, *Champ and a Bit of Sunshine*, *The Red Ghost and a Chocolate Bunny*, *The Loveland Frog and the Narrow Path*, and *Tegan Stone and the Gibson County Beast* - all books in the Texans Investigating Mysterious Entities (T.I.M.E.) cryptozoology and craft beer adventure series.

The Loveland Frog and the Narrow Path is the fourth title in the T.I.M.E. series

Myths and Malts'

Website

Mark Trollinger's

Amazon.com Author Page

WORDS FROM THE AUTHOR

One thing you may notice in this book that differs from the prior three in the series is the removal of the dateline in each chapter. When I started writing Chupacabra, the initial drafts did not have a dateline. In a review, someone mentioned they had difficulty understanding the timeline, so I revised the book to include a clearer picture. One thing that may have gone unnoticed is that every event mentioned in the books occurred on the exact date of the chapter. Every beer listed at a brewery was available on that specific date at that location. At first, it wasn't difficult because I wrote it in real-time, or close to it. However, as life events and general laziness on my part occurred, the period in the real world outpaced the timeline of the fictional work. That made it difficult to research what beer was on tap at a specific brewery four years ago last Friday. Therefore, I decided to remove it and have stories take place in the current time. Here, it is necessary to apply suspension of disbelief because there are still connections between the stories, suggesting they are linear in time.

Another thing I added is a section breaking down the chapters. There are inclusions of facts and maybe points of interest that might go under the radar. Including an annotated section might help with that understanding. I used to love the linear notes in the back of albums or CDs that provided insight into the thoughts of the artists, and that's what I am hoping to display in this area.

I would like to give a few shout outs:

Jo-Ann Holt is the mother of my coworker, Holly. Holly let her mom read the Chupacabra, and she enjoyed it. She asked about book two as well as book three. She is my number one fan, and I am feeling the pressure to finish this fourth book so she can read it.

Thanks also to Eli Watson for taking the time to read the Red Ghost and a Chocolate Bunny. Most of my friends who have served as beta readers are not fans of cryptozoology. I friended Eli on social media and wanted his input because he is a cryptozoology expert. Be sure to check out the podcast he and his friends Alex, and Jasmine put out called Cryptid Campfire. They have a Patreon account where you can learn a lot about from conversations related to cryptozoology. My favorite episode is number 149: Tall Tales #24 The Red Ghost of Arizona. He also has appeared on and produced Chasing Legends and the Beyond the Trail series from Small Town Monsters.

Beer is a big part of this series. We should understand, don't drink and drive. The characters in the series do not go out and get shit-faced, except for Carson when we first meet him the in Chupacabra, but he ended the night in a ride share vehicle. In this book, they have another night on the town in Chapter 2, but again, they have a ride set up ahead of time. Keep in mind, buzzed driving is drunk driving. Make sure you have a designated driver or use a ride share program.

Field Notes

This book is set primarily in Loveland, OH and therefore it made sense to select a Loveland-based non-profit for this book's 15% donation. The Loveland Learning Garden seeks to immerse kids in the outdoors from an early age with the goal of fostering lifelong connections to the wonders of the natural world. Much of this series involves outdoor investigations and the character's connection to the natural world.

If you wish to donate on your own, use the QR Code:

Cover

The cover was created by Nyssa Iniguez, who has worked on the redesign of each cover within the series. It uses a few colors to create a chalk-like feel used by many craft beer breweries in the menus and signage. I call it the craft beer-inspired cover.

Dedication

The book's dedication is the same this time as it is every time: my wife Susana, the kids Karmina and Jorge, my mother, and my grandmother. I also added my great grandparents, Earl and Enid. My great-grandfather used to work at Wright Patterson AFB. This book mentions Commander Williams. His name is Clifford Williams, and that's a tribute to my great-grandfather.

Chapter 1

The book begins with the chapter Little Miami. It introduced us to a new character, Björn Martin, a senior at the University of Cincinnati, working an internship as a bat field technician. I picked this beginning because I have a cousin, Jason, who lives in Cincinnati and had a job that included counting bats. My grandmother, Mary Lou, always got a kick out of the fact his job was to count bats. It wasn't the only aspect of the job, but that's what she remembered and always talked about. Since Jason lives in Cincinnati and had the job, I saw it as a connection to the series. The main characters of T.I.M.E. live in Austin, TX and the bats under the Congress Street Bridge provided the connection to bats in Cincinnati. I knew Loveland Castle would play into the story multiple times, so I picked a location close to it for Björn to conduct his research. I have been to Loveland Castle and there is a large grassy area across from the castle and near the river. I wanted to use that for an encounter and having Björn see the creatures close to there would ensure the investigators would be drawn toward that area.

Chapter 2

For this chapter I wanted the intro to begin with the reader thinking the researchers were going to a speaking event where they would talk about a recent cryptid investigation, but it turns out to be Carson's birthday. I thought there were similarities between a speaking event and a birthday party in the T.I.M.E. universe. • There has been an ongoing tease about jackalopes in books 1, 2, and 3. The restaurant in Austin is called the Jackalope, and it is near the spot where I established the T.I.M.E. offices in book 3. They have a chupacabra burger, and there is another business next door called the Chupacabra cantina. These seemed to fit as the local chapter in the story. • The Shop Beer Company is one of my favorite breweries in Phoenix, and they had a Jackalope beer, which was also quite good. I also enjoy Wren House, and they have a Dreamy Draw beer. It wasn't until my second or third can that I rotated it and saw the spaceship on the backside. Helio Basin was another local brewery, and they had a chupacabra-themed beer. Sadly, they closed in 2020. • The idea for the end of the chapter was based on an observation that certain people love *Wonderwall*, even if they can't sing or play it.

Chapter 3

When I visited the parking area of Loveland Castle, I couldn't go inside because it was closed. I knew I wanted to use it in the story because it is a unique location in the town. Ghost sightings have been reported there, so I created a fictional paranormal team and had them investigate it. Instead of ghosts, they stumble onto the Loveland Frogmen. I wanted to emphasize their experience and credibility so someone would not dismiss it as misidentification or a hoax. I chose the name Porkopolis Paranormal Society because Cincinnati used to be called Porkopolis. I tried to show that although experienced and credible, just because they were familiar with the unknown in terms of ghosts, it may not universally apply to all unknown things, such as cryptids. • I wanted to bring some dark energy affecting Carson to old memories of fighting depression.

Chapter 4

One of the paranormal shows I used to enjoy was *Fact or Faked*. Each member of the team would research a video, then present it at their team meeting. They would vote for two videos to be investigated to determine if it was legitimate or a hoax. I brought that in here with a weekly team meeting at the T.I.M.E. office. It wasn't quite the same because their plan was to have a weekly briefing, but Ty was late because of watching the video filmed by the Porkopolis Paranormal guys. Bringing his laptop to the meeting allowed him to show the video and give a *Fact or Faked* type feel to the chapter. The team watched the video and decided it was something they should investigate. There is a first mention of the files found in the underground Phoenix base in Book 3.

Chapter 5

I spent the first twenty-three years of my life in Ohio, and I did not know there was a Cincinnati subway. My friend Charles Verner sent me a link about the subway via Facebook one day while I was planning the direction for this book. From there I read additional articles about the subway, and I bought the book *Cincinnati's Incomplete Subway: The Complete History (Transportation)* by Jacob R Mecklenborg for additional reading. The idea of urban exploring of abandoned places is interesting, but dangerous.

Remember, do not trespass or break laws.

I know the police patrol the area and they will arrest violators, so don't try this at home. I chose the title Straphanger as it means a standing passenger on a bus, train, subway, and I thought that tied in with the scene taking place in the subway.

Chapter 6

In Chapter three, we had the paranormal team encounter a cryptid. This chapter I wanted to flip it and have the cryptid team encounters a ghost • Bobby Mackey's Music World is a place that I have wanted to visit since seeing it multiple times on Ghost Adventures. I believe it was also on Nick Groff's solo series. My first trip, I made it to the parking lot, but the club has limited hours, so it was closed. In the fall of 2021, I was able to visit while it was open. I didn't see any ghosts that night, but it was a fun night of music at a small honky-tonk bar • I wanted to include some evidence such as the smell of rose perfume and a few EVPs. The glass sliding off at the end was a paranormal sign, but after the investigators left the room without noticing it • I included Rhinegeist as the first local brewery because the name ties into the community, Over-the-Rhine, and *geist* means *ghost*. Their website describes it as a nod to the comeback of the Cincinnati craft beer market. I liked it here, tying into the ghost investigation at Bobby Mackey's. In addition, in 2018, I was supposed to have a book signing there, but it didn't work out.

Chapter 7

I used the title Riverboat Gambler as a tribute to the cardboard boat museum along the river, close to Cincinnati. Throughout this series, the main undertones are cryptozoology and craft beer, but also roadside attractions and pop culture. We also get the meetup between the T.I.M.E. team and the Porkopolis Paranormal team, where we get a discussion on what transpired during the filming of the video.

Chapter 8

The title of the chapter comes from the subway system Vivian explored in chapter five and the Race Street Station • There are more than two churches turned breweries in Cincinnati, but I selected Taft's Ale House and Urban Artifact to model this trend • We also pick up the tip of the creature wearing a bag of some sort. As Tegan speculated, this relates to some of the earlier sightings where witnesses described the Frogmen wearing clothing.

Chapter 9

There are many local words in Cincinnati, or Ohio in general, that are specific to the area. My grandmother Ginny always says *Cincinnatuh,* and family members on both sides say *warsh.* I combined both into the name of the chapter, and then later came up with a scene taking place in the bathroom. • Many of those local words I could attribute in Mango's telling of his experience • I used the name Mango for the character because it is another local word. Growing up, we used to have a garden. One crop we always had was green peppers. My mom called them *mangos.* • We see a man at the bar calling at check in with a Commander Williams.

Chapter 10

I wasn't familiar with the term OODA Loop until I heard it in a meeting at work. A military acronym means *Observe, Orient, Decide, and Act* as a process in decision-making. I thought those fit the process of cryptid investigations. I use the name as the heading chapter and attempted to include each step in the telling of the initial investigation. Another thing I wanted to do here is have the team find clues and plan a hypothesis, but it turns out to be an incorrect one • I introduced a few unique stones that will be explained later in the story.

Chapter 11

The popular idiom phrase is a big fish in a small pond. The Loveland Frogmen are large beings that resemble frogs, so I changed the phrase from fish to frog. We get the team investigating the eyewitness accounts.

Chapter 12

Growing up in Ohio in the 1970s, the Cincinnati Reds were popular. During that time, we knew them as the Big Red Machine. In this chapter, we have Lemmy and the trap used to capture the Loveland Frogmen • I introduced the trap in Chapter 11, but I had him move the trap location and reinforce the trap's design • With the revision of the trap, I decided to note it was red. Being a trap, it could be considered a machine. The chapter title refers to the trap while paying homage to the baseball team I grew up watching.

Chapter 13

This was going to be Chapter 14, but then I moved it to come before the ultimate battle, so the team would know what they were up against • The name of the police chief during the 1955 sightings is accurate and comes from actual events. The man telling the story of the creatures' origins to the investigators is fictional. I wanted to tie the 1955 sightings, the 1972 sightings, and the files found in Phoenix together. Creating a fictional chief of police who was the son of the 1955 chief and had ties to the military and the underground base in Phoenix felt like a good way to combine those • I added Carson dropping a business card at the bar back in chapter 9 and mentioned an elderly man at the bar. Here we learn the elderly police chief was the man at the **bar** • The title comes from the Tex Ritter song, and I used it because I was looking for popular phrases that related to frogs • There is an appearance by Field Agent Garfield Blanchard.

Chapter 14

The chapter name is the same as the name of the musical about the Loveland Frog. I thought the title fit well with what would be the last battle with the frogmen • I tried to change the vibe here as well. The Chief has informed the team in Chapter 13 what these creatures are, and they let their guard down, thinking it was going to be a fun and friendly investigation. I tried to create a darker impression with the storm, the quietness, and a growing sense of negative energy.

Chapter 15

The final in each book has always included a reflection about the investigation and some minor clue that ties into the next story. This time we learn Tegan is struggling with the last battle and has reached a decision on her future. We learn her feelings not only relate to the events here in Book 4, but they started in Book 3 with the discovery of the underground lab and spaceship • There were a couple of clues in this chapter for what is coming next. While setting up the beginning ideas that would lead into book five, I had an idea for another story. In writing the first few lines of Book 5, I felt there was more between the end of this book and the start of the next. I put Book 5 on hold and wrote a solo adventure for Tegan that fits into that space. That is the next story in this arc. I didn't want to call it Book 5, so internally here at the Casa de Chupacabra, I call it four and a half • Again we see Field Agent Garfield Blanchard. This time, he leaves a message for Commander Williams and appears to be familiar with the Xeephines.

Epilogue

After the team heads back to Austin without Tegan. I intended this to wrap up her recovery and thought process after the events of Chapter 14. This will send her in a new direction. The team will continue into Book 5, but Tegan will become a separate storyline and star in her own solo book. As a reader, you could follow the team into Book 5, but there will be some things that may not be clear unless you read the solo story.

Beer List

This is an inclusion at the end of each book. It is a list of the brewery, name, and style of every beer mentioned in the book. Think of it as a checklist if you are up for the challenge of trying the beers herewithin. As stated at the beginning of the book, these beers are not meant to be an endorsement. There are certainly excellent beers in the regional markets that are not included. It is used to add realism to the story.

When I travel, I usually seek out local breweries and try a variety of beers. When selecting beers to be included in each book, the number one factor is location. If there is a great brewery but it doesn't fit with the story's direction, I will skip it and find one that is located in the general area of where the story is at that time.

A second factor is character style preference. From the beginning of the series I have attempted to show Carson enjoys imperial stouts, Ty likes the smoky flavor of a rauchbier (but he is open to other styles as that is not a commonly offered style at most breweries), Kareem loves an IPA: single, double, triple, New England, West Coast, it doesn't matter. He loves them all. In addition, Tegan enjoys the Berliner Weisse (although she can also get down with a gose).

My next deciding factor in the book, much like in real life, is the name. If it has an interesting name, I am usually buying it.

Photo Challenge

Another way I wanted to make this series interactive was to use one of those daily photo challenges consisting of a word or phrase related to the book. Readers could post a daily photo to their Instagram page with the hashtag **#chupacabradailyphotochallenge** and we could see what other readers are posting. I will start this up in January 2022. Check out my Instagram page for details: **mark_trollinger.**

 # Recommendations

Have you ever accidentally become part of a community? That's what I feel I have done with these books. Years ago, I never imagined writing books, especially about cryptozoology and craft beer. However, I wrote Chupacabra and then started getting more involved in groups and stories related to cryptozoology. Now I feel like I am part of the group and I try to promote others who are doing it too. A few pages I recommend on Instagram:

Strange Little Lands: I have purchased three of these little diorama scenes. Each one is reasonably prices and excellently crafted. These incredible works of art have a cryptozoology theme. You won't be sorry with any purchase here.

Cryptid Comfort I love seeing the handcrafted stuffed toys that she makes. She is touring again, and I recommend looking at her schedule and trying to find a show to support these wonderful creations.

Cryptid Campfire: Mentioned in the acknowledgements with Eli Watson, this is a wonderful podcast. They cover so many topics related to cryptozoology. Support the Patreon channel and you get some early access.

Cryptid Crate: I worked this one into the story where Carson is wearing a shirt. I love this box and have been a subscriber for a while. My book, *The Chupacabra*, was included in the box a couple of years ago. Moreover, Derek Hayes is a great guy.

Mr. Cryptozoology: His page I discovered recently, but what a lot of research. He introduced a lot of cryptids, urban legends, and interesting stories. I have learned a lot about creatures I didn't know before.

Strang.ology I love the merch he makes here. I especially like the pins, shirts, and patches that feature a cryptid from specific states. I have purchased a pin of the Loveland Frog, the Chupacabra, and of Champ. He also has a podcast I recommend checking out.

Lurk the Game: This is an upcoming project, but there is a Facebook page and a group to join. It will be a Kickstarter project, but right now, it is in the development stages. I am already excited and joined the page. It is cool seeing the different cryptids as they are announced. At one time I thought about making a cryptozoology and craft beer board game, and while I did sketch it out, I wasn't sure how to even start with it, so that is likely a shelved idea.

Selfie Locations

If you picked up the reissue of the *Chupacabra*, *Champ*, or the *Red Ghost*, you are familiar with this section of mentioned selfie locations throughout the book. I recommend you take a selfie at these locations and upload to social media sites using **#chupacabraselfiechallenge** to build a community and make it more realistic. Even though only book was about the chupacabra, it has become a mascot of the entire series.

If you missed the locations in the story, here is a list including in this book:

> Saddled jackalope at The Jackalope (Austin, TX)
>
> Chupacabra Cantina (Austin, TX)
>
> Large wooly mammoth (Cincinnati/Northern Kentucky airport)
>
> Bobby Mackey's (Wilder, KY)
>
> Three-way @ Skyline Chili (multiple locations)
>
> Chateau Laroche aka Loveland Castle (Loveland, OH)

 # Sound Booth

I spend a lot of time listening to music when I write. During the writing of this book, I spent a lot of time listening to:

Snotty Nose Rez Kids – they have a song that is a recent release called Wild Boy. It mentions several times Bukwus, a supernatural spirit also called wild man of the woods. Sounds a little like a cryptid.

Deap Vally – I first heard of this group a few years ago while attending a music festival here in Phoenix. They are good. My favorite song by them is Royal Jelly.

L.A. Witch – The name of this genre appears to be garage-rock. I first encountered them while listening to other bands listed here and it played once it hit the similar music portion following the videos I had lined up. I was able to see them live in October 2020 and recommend them.

The Darts (US) – Another all-female band, this time from Phoenix and in the Garage-rock-psych rock genre. Their Facebook page describes them as, *"If Elvira and Wednesday Adams consumed the flesh of man, drank shots of snake venom, started a band."* I mean, how could you not listen? In addition, the bass lines are incredible.

Continuing the tradition of the first three books, this one also has a Spotify playlist.

Loveland Frog Spotify Playlist

www.ingramcontent.com/pod-product-compliance
Lightning Source LLC
Chambersburg PA
CBHW051508150726
47997CB00001B/165